Letters Between Us

Linda Rader Overman

Plain View Press
P. O. 42255
Austin, TX 78704

plainviewpress.net
sb@plainviewpress.net
1-512-441-2452

Cover art and design by Michael Overman.

Contents

Acknowledgments

To Deva, for her unceasing love and encouragement, Michael for his magical and passionate artistry, Dr. Carolyn Maher for her insistence to continue, and Henriette Balague', my mother, for always reminding me to trust.

To my husband, Jim, for everything.

Special thanks to my keen-eyed copy editor, Gregory Wright, who misses nothing. To my early readers and mentors, Lynn Stine, Cheryl Smith, and Phyllis Gebauer.

To Susan Bright for affirming my belief in this work.

To Kip, my muse.

Prologue

This journey could have started differently, but the fact is that it didn't. It started at the end, and even though it became obvious that that was the beginning, in the long run there was nothing anyone could have done to change that.

Or was there?

Santa Barbara Herald
Friday/July 7, 1989

MISSING MOTHER FOUND DEAD IN DUMPSTER

By Dan Delgado
Santa Barbara Herald Staff Writer

The body of a woman identified as Katharine Taylor Fields, 39, was discovered in a trash bin at the Cold Spring Tavern Inn near Lake Cachuma Thursday evening, the Santa Barbara County Sheriff's Department reported today. The discovery was made by a family who had stopped at the inn after hours to use its restroom.

Fields had disappeared from a picnic at Lake Cachuma on Tuesday for patients of Santa Barbara Psychiatric Hospital, where she had been hospitalized for the past eight months following a nervous breakdown.

Mrs. A. DeFrancisco, who discovered the body, said, "I thought someone had pitched a life-sized doll in the trash. She reminded me of Sleeping Beauty with her long blonde hair and pale skin. She had such a peaceful smile on her face."

David Fields, 42, of Fields Auto Repair, confirmed the identity of the body and also identified himself as her estranged husband. Mrs. Fields leaves behind a daughter Jillian, 6. Cause of death as yet to be determined. Pending funeral arrangements are under the direction of the Lee Funeral Home.

Chapter One:
The Best Of Friends

"You just want to send me to hell."

"No, Mom, you're doing that all by yourself." My hand starts to strangle the receiver.

"What have I done to you that you hate me so much?" Damn it, I almost cut myself trying to slice tomatoes for dinner, balance the phone, and swallow two Advil and one Tylenol with a gulp of cold coffee.

"I don't have any food in the house," Mom insists. I pull the phone away from my ear momentarily. I want to throw it on the floor and smash it, but I don't. Instead, I can feel a familiar heat spreading from my neck and flushing my face. This always happens when I get mad. I gather my annoying shoulder-length hair off my neck and throw it up into a ponytail with the rubber band that was holding the celery together.

"Mom, what are you talking about, Ana always makes you a nice dinner. You told me you liked her cooking." I jack up the air conditioning. The temperature in Encino today is in its usual July high 90s and inside the house the thermostat reads 82. I should have turned it on this morning, but I always think it's best to conserve energy, and then I regret it around 4 o'clock. My temples are throbbing.

"I don't eat *her* awful food." Mom's rant continues, "I'm not so stupid, dumb and blind like you tell everybody—"

"If you don't like your live-in, then I'm putting you in a home." I have to repeat myself three more times. Mom's so deaf these days I have to shout. I hate pulling the put-you-in-a-home card, but I have no choice. Hearing loss, macular degeneration, and Alzheimer's make my 78-year-old former powerhouse of a mother almost unrecognizable. Confrontational, disagreeable, nasty—all her native negative qualities are exacerbated by this horrendous disorder. It's as if the loving woman who was my supportive rock died five years ago. Now all it takes, sometimes, is one inane question: "Hi Mom, how are you doing, where is Ana taking you to lunch today?"

"Oh, so you want to put me in jail now, is that it?" she barks.

"I'm not having this conversation with you!" I slam down the phone. This is our daily scenario, *if* Mom is in her Alzheimer paranoid-bitch-on-wheels mood. Other times, she talks sweetly to me code switching, as we have always done, between her native language and

English: "You are so wonderful, *mija*. You work so hard, *pobrecita*, I know I'm being, uhhh being, *como se dice* . . . difficult." But those days of kindness and clarity are disappearing. And as the months have passed she's begun an odd form of self-inflicted torment that requires regular clipping of her fingernails almost to the quick, which does no good. But I don't want to think about that now.

The phone rings again, but I don't want to answer it. I'm sure it's Mom gunning for me, ready to spew more dementia-infused venom. The ring persists. John says I shouldn't answer the phone when she keeps calling, but I do anyway. All right, for God sakes, all right. I wipe my hands, fill my coffee cup and sit down at the table. I might as well get some more caffeine in me for the next round.

When I first hear David's voice on the phone, I say I'm glad to hear from him, which I'm not. I never liked him, but at this moment he sounds like he's been crying. I ask him how Katharine is doing, afraid of the answer.

"It's pretty bad, Laura," he says.

"How bad can it be?" I ask, never imagining the worst. I know the worst is possible, but I don't want to believe it would or could occur. "When—" Then I hear, "passed away yesterday morning . . ." That's all I hear. David is talking but I'm stuck on "passed away." Disjointed phrases spill so fast that I can't grasp them all at once. He stops and then silence, and then more fragments. Something about Katharine in a garbage container. He pauses, breathes and continues.

"Sheriff thinks she was probably walking along the highway, at first, but then why wasn't she—" I still can't get beyond, "Katharine passed away yesterday morning." What . . . what? How did she pass? Did she have to try hard or was it easy? She passed away yesterday morning, alone. Life snuffed out of her while she passed away.

All I can think of is when the two of us were in junior high school and Katharine passed her science test and I didn't, even though I tried cheating off of her. "Laura," she announced jumping up and down, "I passed with an A-, if only I hadn't missed number 20, I would have gotten an A!" Katharine loved studying. I didn't bother. Passing with high grades brought Katharine joy. School for me was simply a place to meet cute boys.

But now Katharine's passing bears a shroud weighted by the trash of civilized disposal: rotting food, torn paper, dirty plastic cups, old Pepsi and 7-Up cans, and shards of broken glass. Icons of useful disuse, misuse, and discards of wastefulness enfold an emaciated, anguished, depressed, and dirty Katharine—dead when the police found her, all thirty-nine years of her in a graffiti-ridden beige Dumpster.

After hanging up the phone, I lay my head on the pine kitchen table and stare at the wall with its white painted-over pine paneling that I hate—the paint, not the pine. In front of me I focus on the salt and pepper shakers: antique crystal and silver. Next to them is a sterling silver breadbasket filled with table napkins. I take my hand and sweep it across the table. The napkins and the basket and the antique shakers fly across the room. I stand up and see the shakers broken into many pieces on the tile floor. Funny—didn't hear anything hit the ground. I kneel down and examine the sterling silver tops—bent and slightly misshapen. The napkins lie like fallen snow next to them; the breadbasket is upside down and undamaged. Wonder what my mother-in-law would think if she saw this right now—these were her birthday gifts to me. What would my husband say? John, where is he? At the studio in one of the usual meetings . . . don't want to talk yet.

I throw on a short sun dress and some platforms (too hot for tight jeans), exchange the celery rubber band for a large hair clip, and leave the house as I can't stand the silence. While driving around, tears pour down my face. The tears combine with my sweat to form rivulets down my neck dripping between my breasts. Summers in the San Fernando Valley are long and hot—even all the oak trees providing elegant shade can't abate the relentless heat. My thighs singe from the burning leather car seat as I pull down my hem for protection. The cool air blowing from the air conditioning vent can't work fast enough.

I pull into Fashion Square in Sherman Oaks and march into Bullocks. I find myself in the lingerie department. Silk lingerie on sale: 25% off. Yes, I'll buy two of everything in black, pink, and red. I spend $400 and return home. I stuff the bag of purchases into the closet and there it sits. Don't remember why I have that large bag in the closet sitting on top of my shoes. It's just there. *I'm* just there, sitting on the bed staring at it.

The sunlight reflects something bright white in John's dresser mirror. I turn around and see Katharine's last letter, written three months earlier. It still sits folded on my roll-top desk, partially stuffed inside one of the little boxes in the middle. On a sheet of grey paper in an uneven hand, as if she couldn't focus, but was in a hurry to get down the words, Katharine wrote:

Santa Barbara Psychiatric still...

Dear Laura,

Have I told you what I cannot . . . have never told. It's not so much in words that I am lacking to tell you. I wanted to tell you everything, but I prefer sleep, that eternal parent that beckons . . . ~~don't know how much longer I can~~

Want you to have the letters in case.

David and I will probably have stopped talking by the time you read them. He refuses to bring Jillian anymore . . . Dr. Powers says it's better for now as time is what I need. Jillian needs . . . ~~David needs.~~ Maybe you can help Jillian understand someday. Hope you saved all of your letters and journals. We promised each other we would never stop writing. WE WOULD NEVER throw them out, didn't we? You will know when to read . . . I don't know anymore except that I love you . . . remember.

"The dark takes form of the white and reveals it."

Can't recall who wrote this just now, but do this for me because I can't.

April weather keeps raining inside and out

Rain inside and out . . .

Katharine

I waited for the letters to arrive, but they never did. I called Katharine at the hospital on the designated patient pay phone, which was either busy or, when another patient answered, Katharine couldn't come to the phone. It was never clear why. So my letters went unanswered as did my phone calls, but then came her last phone call and I knew she was lost.

O

I drive into the church parking lot. It's still deserted, but for one car. I'm early, and walk inside. At the entrance I pick up an announcement card from a short stack that reads:

In Memory Of	Katharine Isabel Taylor
Born	Fort Lewis, Washington
	October 21, 1949
Passed Away	Santa Barbara, California
	July 6, 1989
Services	Santa Barbara Unitarian Church
	111 S. Obispo
	Santa Barbara, California
	Thursday, July 13, 1989
	9:00 a.m.
Officiant	Reverend Michael Keyes

Sitting down in a pew, I feel the coolness of the church rush into my body. It's so quiet in here. There's no music, no people. I'm alone for the moment. The drive north from Los Angeles was a quick one, less than the usual hour-and-a-half. David's description of Katharine's final moments—hours perhaps—replays in my head.

"She disappeared from the hospital," he said, "two days before."

"Why?"

"I'm not real sure, but she just walked away. The details are still sketchy."

"Was it suicide?"

"Don't know yet. An autopsy will take four to six weeks."

Katharine's final phone call to me echoes even louder in my brain: "I'm evil, Laura, evil. I'm the devil and I need to die. I need to be punished."

"Please Katharine, honey, stop it."

"I'm the devil incarnate and I'm going to punish . . . punish her—"

"Look, sweetie, you remember what I told you once about suicide? What happens when you kill yourself and wake up on the other side?" Mom had always told me that suicide was a shortcut to a death solely planned by God. If you took it, your soul would be stuck somewhere between heaven and earth, earthbound she called it. There it had to wait until the actual year, month, day, minute, and second arrived of your destined moment of death, and only then could your soul progress to the other side. Where you went depended on the way you lived your life on earth. It was one of the things she told me in childhood that I still believed. Mom does not remember telling me this anymore, but I have never forgotten it.

"Dead . . . should be . . . will be dead. Evil. David says so. Everybody says so. I scare Jillian. I must be punished."

"Katharine, Kitty, listen to me, just listen—"

"The devil says I belong—dead."

"Remember what I said about ending your life before it's your time—"

"I shouldn't have done it, shouldn't have slept with . . . I'm bad, responsible you know, for all of it. Wha . . .what? No . . . I've got to go; they're making me hang up now."

"Katharine, I love you." Silence. "Katharine, I love you."

"I love you too." Click.

This was not the girl I had known since junior high school any longer. She was not the best friend I loved like a sister any longer. She was not the supportive lifelong friend who knew everything about me any longer. The gentle, reassuring, sweet mother to her baby girl I had known was gone. She was someone else, a vacant Katharine who at the same time was possessed by another. How did she get to this place and to such an end?

I arrived at Katharine's home this morning, following the memorial service. Almost every corner brought forth her presence even though she had not lived there for many months. Her Charles Keane and Rosamond prints were still up in the hall; her English pine and glass bookcase remained in the living room although empty of her books; her needlepoint throw pillows of cats and tigers still lay on the beige leather sofa with Geo and Squashy purring nearby seemingly oblivious of the group of people invading their feline space. It seemed like Katharine could walk in any minute to greet her mourners who packed the tiny house.

I took a look at her daughter playing in her room with her cousins. The little girl turned around and there was Katharine, staring back at me. Jillian wore the outfit John and I had given her for Christmas; a buffed cotton pink-flowered dress cut out at the back, accented with a pink satin bow and ruffled collar with white leather ankle-strap shoes adorned with white satin and rhinestone bows. She *is* Katharine almost, with a sameness yet a differentness: the almond-shaped intense blue eyes, honeyed blonde hair, a quiet and observing nature, but not that sad, bewildered, and longing countenance of Katharine's. Today her translucent skin was flushed with the pink of intense child's play.

Jillian's auburn-haired cousins, seven and eight years old, were helping her search for Barbie's Ken so he could take Barbie to a party. I slowly approached her.

"Hi, Jillian, can I help?"

"We need Ken, we can't find him and we need him," she pleaded. Smiling up at me, she asked, "Can you help Lori and Jeannie and me find him?"

Spying Ken's foot on the bed, I said, "I think if you look underneath that pillow on your bed, you might just—" Jillian quickly turned around as Lori reached under the bed pillow.

"Bad boy, Ken, hiding like that, thank goodness we found you!" Jeannie admonished Ken. Jillian shook her finger at the doll.

I told Jillian how beautiful she looked and asked if she remembered who'd given her the outfit she was wearing. "You did!" she announced with her head bent over as she examined Barbie with small delicate hands.

"And who am I?" It had been almost a year since I'd last seen her.

"Don't *you* know? You're Laura, Mommy's friend," Jillian said with a giggle, looking at me as if I were the child and she the adult. Her two cousins bickered over what Ken should wear on his date, a suit or his jogging outfit.

"Yes, you're right," I said, "Mommy was my best friend and I loved her very much."

"My mommy's in heaven and I miss her," Jillian said while she changed Barbie from her bathing suit into a party dress. I gave this littlest angel a squeeze.

"I miss her too, darling."

As I held Jillian, a vision came to me of the small bundle of life I once carried within my body, and never had the opportunity to hold. I shoved the thought away and gently released my grip on Jillian's soft and smell-of-sunshine body. I left Jillian to her playmates and her child's world of make-believe. Soon enough she'd discover the elusiveness of such a world and the true meaning of today's loss.

David and I were talking in a corner of the kitchen—a kitchen that appeared newly remodeled, with a freshly plastered wall where the door to the shop office used to be. Something Katharine had wanted David to do three years earlier. I could still hear her grumbling about having the auto shop garage open right into the kitchen. "If David would just close off the shop from the house, then the mechanics wouldn't keep coming in and out and messing up the place and spilling coffee everywhere."

The kitchen had a window of glass brick over a new sink, a Sub-Zero refrigerator, a Gaggenau stove, a new white linoleum tile floor, butter yellow painted cabinets, and a small black granite counter shared with the dining area that gave the room the openness Katharine wanted, yet the separateness from the business she had craved.

"Katharine never wanted me to spend any money on a new kitchen while she was here. She was afraid of the expense, so I waited until she moved out to do it," David said as he walked over to the refrigerator. He pulled out a beer and twisted off the cap.

"It looks wonderful," I lied. Katharine hated painted cabinets. Just like me.

"I bartered a contractor for it when I worked on about six of his trucks," he said rather proudly. "I finished it a few weeks before . . . before she—" he hesitated and gulped down the Bud.

"I'm sure she would have loved it," I lied again. Katharine would have preferred tile counters because she hated granite and glass brick, thought they looked too much like Lego sets.

"I was trying to finish it before Jillian's seventh birthday and now I can't even think of doing a party for her. Katharine and I had talked *way* earlier, but . . . "

I looked at this man who had lived with her for almost twenty years, who nursed her through relapses of depression, who supposedly loved her, but abruptly cut her out of his life, and Jillian's. I looked at David's well-worn hands, dirt no doubt under those large fingernails, hands that repaired broken cars and regenerated the weary machines with new life—but why not also Katharine? He appeared shaken by her passing, but I couldn't help wondering why he'd made her leave. Why had he insisted so vehemently on a separation when she seemed to need him the most?

David finally offered me a beer. I declined as people came up to him to express their sympathies inside this cheerful, but empty-of-Katharine's-touch kitchen. He introduced me as the girl who'd grown up with Katharine. People smiled, politely. I didn't know very many of them. I knew some of the family, but most of these people had worked with Katharine or were parents she'd known from Jillian's school.

I saw one strange, clearly distracted young Hispanic woman with short black hair and a plain black dress, slightly overweight, standing within earshot. She appeared uncomfortable and out of place, holding a crumpled yellow tissue in her hand. She cried silently. I couldn't tell if she was alone or not. When she heard we'd been friends, she came over to me.

"It's my fault, I should have stayed with her. It's all my fault." Her tone was despairing.

"What's your name?" I asked.

"Maria," she answered, "I should have watched her, it's all my fault, it's all my fault . . ." A fairly nondescript man I hadn't noticed before guided her away and they quickly left. I asked David who she was.

"Not sure, probably someone who was in the hospital with Katharine, you know what I mean?"

I walked out of the front door to see if I could catch her, but Maria and the man had vanished. What did she mean? I walked back into the kitchen hoping David might shed further light on this sad young woman. When we were left alone again he dismissed the subject.

"My new girlfriend is a lot like Katharine; some of my friends tell me she even looks a little like her," he said in a low voice. His admission felt like a ton of bricks falling on my head.

"Did Katharine know?" I asked, still in shock.

"Yes, and . . well . . .she accepted it," he said. David was a God damn liar, I didn't believe it.

If Katharine accepted David's divided love, then why in some of our few last rational discussions was she so upset that David wouldn't take her back?

"Laura, he was going to take me back, he *was*, then we made love, and, and then I told him about the affair with the man at work and, and he started to cry and said he couldn't do it, that he was done. He just kept saying that awful word—done." Her voice pitched with unsteady breathiness, her words gave way to sobs. My absorption in this memory hadn't heard David change the subject.

" . . . you know, every time she came back from visiting you, she'd give me a hard time. It'd take me months to turn her way of thinkin' back 'round!" All these years of our tolerating each other for Katharine's sake and now he finally said it.

"It was hard for me to watch Katharine allow you to treat her like a doormat. It may have been her choice, but I didn't have to like it," I responded.

He disagreed that he was ever, in any large part, responsible for Katharine's unhappiness. He felt she worried too much about money and did not support him when he made financial commitments to expand the business even though it put them both further in debt. I wanted to take a swing at him.

"David," I said, holding myself back, "if anything, I was her friend and I was loyal to her and loved her with all my heart. Did you really love her? Did you?" Cold anger was turning to pouring tears.

"We both did," he answered, his eyes watering also. On impulse, I reached up, wanting to slug him and hug him at the same time, but I just let my hand drop. I noticed he'd gained a lot of weight and his khaki-colored shirt fit tightly around his shoulders. Even after a wake David smelled like his garage. Katharine used to say that no matter how much David washed, his cologne was hard to miss: Valvoline 10W-40.

Someone we both loved was dead and we just stood there for a minute looking down at the floor, hoarding that love and hurt. A couple of mourners approached to say good-bye. David walked them to the door. I felt awkward and poured myself a cup of coffee. David came back and took another swig from his beer.

"Laura," he said, clearing his throat, "go on upstairs in the bedroom . . . and . . . you'll find a brown cardboard box with some of Katharine's mementos from childhood. You know how she saved everything, and besides she said once they were for you. I think there are some pictures of you two and . . . well . . . I haven't gone through it yet, but . . . go on." He saw my face light up. Was he really saying this to me? This guy who disliked me as much as I did him?

"Go on," he coaxed.

As I walked through the living room toward the stairs I noticed there was not one picture of Katharine anywhere, not on a table, not on a wall, not in Jillian's room. Hurrying up the stairs I heard snippets of conversations from the wives of some of David's employees, and his sister-in-law.

"Towards the end it got so bad, she was calling me constantly."

"I'd run out of the house when the phone would ring, because I knew it was her and I didn't wanna answer."

"I'd tell her, every day is a new day, Katharine; you gotta take one day at a time man, you know."

"It was hard to take those phone calls and her going on and on, but I couldn't hang up on her, I couldn't."

I felt more depressed with each comment and each step.

At the last step, I remembered that the small upstairs was the entire bedroom. Straight in front of me was an empty space under the slanted ceiling, flooded with sunlight from the skylight above, that had contained Katharine's writing desk. Near the bed, I saw the file box brightened by the white Tensor lamp on the rush chair that functioned as a night stand. On the box were the words "Photos and Things" in brown marker, in the handwriting I had grown to know so well. I wanted to rip it open, but checked my impulse as I knelt down on the taupe carpet and slowly opened the lid. Inside was a mound of papers, writings, photos, and the smell of teenage-long-ago. I lifted out one old letter written on three-holed wide-lined school paper marked with folds and creases. I unfolded it and . . . it was in my own handwriting. My God! She saved the letters from school too. I rose up, sat on the edge of the bed and began to read:

8ᵀᴴ grade

Dear catherine (or is it katharine?),

I didn't mean to wipe my hands on your skirt. They were all wet and it's such a long skirt that i thought you wouldn't notice my using a little corner dumb, huh?

Isn't sewing class a real drag. I can't sew so my mom does it for me. Our teacher mrs. williams is sooo b-o-r-i-n-g. Write me back, ok? Maybe we could be frends friends? Pretty please, with sugar on top.

I am 12 going on 13, how old are you?
Your new friend and pal (i hope)

Laura wells

8ᵀᴴ grade

Dear katharine,
    I decided the best name for you from now on is k-i-t, since
that's your initials, besides kitty fits you perfectly and your
~~blond~~ blonde and your blue eyed just like my sweet kitty at home.
It'll be our special name for you. Kitty—everybody will start
calling you that. I've already told joy to.
    Hey, can you sleep over this weekend? My mom says it's ok,
ok? It's really groovy sharing lockers.
    Your new and favorite friend,
    Laura

    P.S. Why did president kennedy have to die? I cried all
through geography. The teachers said to stay off the phones but i'll
try to call you tonight anyhow.

    This letter is confidential and only to be opened on pain of
death!!!
    9Th grade

    Hey kitty,
    We're going to palm springs for xmas vacation and guess
what? Mom says you can come too!! Out-of-sight, huh!! Ask your
mom, okay? We can read this book together after mom goes to bed.
I borrowed it from joy, it's called peyton place by grace metalious
and it's really bitchin! Joy passed it to me in history class today.
Everybody's reading it. Everybody that's in that is.
    Joy wrapped it in a plain brown book cover, because if miss
marca or anyone else caught on— it'd be straight to the vp's office.
Joy says she took it from her parent's library, but she'd be in big
trouble if they knew. It has some really far out parts in it where

22

they do...Well you know...and they do –you know – in detail!

What do you think about what mom said about tampax making you loose your virginity? Darcy parker says that's bullshit. She uses it and she's still a virgin. I think?!

Wuv ya, & definitely a virgin,
Laura

P.S. Joy is lending me catcher in the rye next!

10Th grade

Dear kitty,

It was me calling you last night, but mom grabbed the phone out of my hands just as you answered. She is ready to ground me for life and from using the phone. I stole some barrettes from the ranch market next door to us, yesterday, and got busted by an undercover cop. Damn! I had the money to pay for `em, but god, it was only $1.39 For a pack of three, big deal. Anyway, the cop and the store manager tried to freak me out and say, maybe they should take me downtown and put me in juvey hall. I really started crying, then i was scared shitless.

After mom got the call she started in on me with:

"In my life i have never stolen a thing, my god how could you? You're not poverty stricken, you only have to ask for what you want. What's the matter with you? (She's really shrieking now) i work like a slave to keep the family going and pay for this house, the food, your clothes and this is what you do?!" Then she goes into more of the i-am-disappointed-in-you speech. Brother i just wanted to see if i could get away with it? It didn't seem like such a big deal. I blew it didn't i? You'll still be my best friend, won'tcha?

Mom says you can't stay over on the weekends, either, for at least a month!! I can't even go to any of the dances at school.

I'll go crazy, i know it. And god, maybe i should consider. Suicide? I feel like a prisoner, cooped up in this house with mimi, a grandmother who needs to be cleaned up after, like a baby. Who gets that job? Me, of course. When i get home from school there's a trail from her bedroom to the bathroom where she didn't quite make it on time. The floor heater is in her path and does it ever stink when we turn it on now. God, i wish mimi was dead or else mom would put her in a home.

Forget that, mom says:

"I'll never put my mother in a home. This is her home. My father left it to her when he died. How could you say such a thing?"

"Easy," i go, "you're at the restaurant working all the time so i get stuck scrubbing shit off the walls and floors of a senile 88 year old woman."

She slaps me across the mouth and goes, "my mother is not senile. Don't you dare use that word!"

"I wish she was dead and i wish you were dead!" I yell back at her and she smacks me again and i couldn't stand it so i hit her back. Then she goes back to her damn restaurant.

I hate that place. Mom says i'll have to start working there over school vacations since she can't trust me to be alone anymore. Life is the shits.

Love, totally miserable,

Laura

July 13, 1989
Vista del Mar Inn
Santa Barbara
9:02 p.m.

David looked puzzled when I finally told him I had taken a room at this hotel. I told him how much it meant to me to sift through the "photos" of Katharine and me as kids and that I wanted to spend some quiet time going over them. If he didn't object, I'd return the box by the end of the week. Surprisingly, he had allowed me to take it. He said he wasn't ready to go through it just yet, so, if I found there was anything really important to let him know. Actually I haven't the slightest idea at this point what his definition of important is, but definitely not the past of his dead wife. He has moved into the future with another while leaving Katharine and her mental illness behind.

"Probably just a lot of girl stuff in there," David smirked as I left the house. God what a jerk!

"Probably," I answered, smiling a hairsprayed-on smile.

O

This is the key that will unlock the door into the past of two lives that beg to be rediscovered. A journey, I did not realize until this moment, I've been longing for. I need the rest of this newfound key to continue.

John should be home from the studio by now.

"Hi, I'm staying here for a while."

"What . . . oh thank God, I thought it was your mom again. What . . . wait a minute . . . how long?"

"Until it feels right to leave."

There was a silence, then, "Laura, you're not yourself. It's Katharine's death. It's affected you more than you realize—"

"John, listen, I need you to do me a favor. You know that box I keep wrapped up with that old frayed purple ribbon?"

"No."

"Yes you do, it's the one shoved up on the top shelf of the linen closet."

"Yeah, what about it?"

"I want you to messenger it to me tomorrow."

"What? I thought you said it was full of a bunch of old junk from school."

"It is and it isn't . . . I need it. Please, it's important!"

"I thought you were in such a big rush to send something off to Outside/Inside Books. In fact, some woman called yesterday and left a message . . . something about a winter or spring issue . . . I think . . . whatever."

"Was it Sherry?" I drummed my fingers on the table.

"Uh, maybe Cheryl or Sharon . . . no . . . Sherry. Yeah Sherry." I drummed harder.

"Christ, why can't you just write it down when you listen to the message? God, this is getting old!"

"Hey come on now, you know they're all the same to me."

"Oh yes, dear, I know. Believe me, I know." Just once I wished we could talk about my writing as if he gave a shit.

"It's been a very long day," I said. "I've got to get to bed."

"Call me, okay? Let me know when you're coming home. And—this is a minor detail, I know—but what about . . . us, here, house in the suburbs. Oh God, and those phone calls from your mom?"

"I don't know," I said softly, and hung up.

○

Now, I sit staring at the box of letters. What has happened to John and me, I'm not sure. After twelve years I don't care. I'll think about it tomorrow; tonight I need to dream. Katharine, if you were here, we could talk about it just like we used to talk about things when we were schoolgirls. Staying up all night. Lying on our backs. Heads nestled on our pillows staring up at the ceiling, that powder-blue bedroom ceiling in my mom's room with the matching powder-blue Princess phone with the lighted dial. I thought I'd arrived with that phone, but I hated having to share a bedroom with my mom. But it never bothered Katharine. Mom was usually asleep and snoring anyway. God, would Katharine and I laugh, giggle until we both had to practically pee in our underwear.

When we passed notes in school we'd laugh so hard that we'd raise our hands simultaneously for the hall pass to the bathroom. The teachers usually liked Katharine better than me since she was the good student, nothing ever lower than an A-. I was the fuck-up, everything lower than a B-, so she always got picked before I did. I had to wait until she came back. Once I found a note stuck to the mirror in the bathroom. And I have found again, in Katharine's brown cardboard box:

laura.

they paved paradise and put up a parking lot.

love joni mitchell. oooooooo ya ya ya ya.

Chapter Two:
Just Us Girls

Laura Wells' Journal

July 14, 1989
Vista del Mar Inn
Santa Barbara
2:57 p.m.

There's a knock at my door, it's late afternoon. I've been asleep all day because it eluded me all night. A commuter train has a habit of barreling by just behind the hotel around 6 a.m., then half past noon, and then again around 6:17 p.m. So, I can always count on it as an unwanted alarm clock, but not today.

I throw on a robe and open the door. I smell the sea. Seagulls sound their calls. Waves break persistently in the still bright and blue day. My eyes wince at the glare reflecting off of the sand, and the ocean front boardwalk where couples stroll by past my room. It's the studio messenger—smiling white pearly teeth, a young twenty—they usually are. He adjusts his shades. I adjust my robe. He hands me my box—the box with the purple ribbon still on it. I'm grateful John didn't remove it. The messenger puts it on the floor next to the other box. They're practically the same size. Katharine's looks a little more beaten up than mine—just two simple tan cardboard boxes holding other times and other lives within. He leaves amidst my thank you's—oh thank you, thank you. I tip him ten dollars.

I open the box with "School Correspondence" in bold black marker on it. With a knife from last night's meal, I have to score the seams several times before they give way to the dullness of it. My stomach is doing a dance, a hard-driving twist. Out onto the floor spills wide-lined paper from those early school days, hundreds of sheets covered with Katharine's hard-to-read writing. It took a whole semester for me to learn to read it with ease. Her script was small and her letters were never completely formed, as if she was giving hints as much as writing her mind. To comprehend it was a right that had to be earned through the struggle of understanding Katharine's whole being and the true impression it was actually making. Something I am still mastering. Underneath all of that correspondence is an array of photographs taken of us through the years by each other, by friends, or by my uncle Bernie, who worked as a photographer in Hollywood chasing after stars and starlets at movie premieres.

I sit on the floor between these two harbingers of childhood and lift out the sheets of wide-lined, thin-lined, and unlined paper with flashes of blue, black, lavender, red, and turquoise ink from each box. Squiggles and swirls of handwriting—accounts, affections and sentiments— underscored by 3x3 snapshots, 3x5 prints, and 8x10 glossies, black-and-white and in color. Some of the letters look as pristine and unwrinkled as the day they were written, while others appear to have been folded or crumpled up and then smoothed back out again as an afterthought. Some are still in envelopes, most are not. I realize this is the closest I will ever come to physically touching Katharine again; touching what she herself has touched, while reading her thoughts and almost hearing her voice. Tears course down my cheeks as I slowly pass my fingers across the pieces of paper, caressing the cursive and trying to absorb an energy, a quintessence that was once Katharine, once shared by me—both of us just a couple of kids trying to survive the innocence of their puerile youth and not be buried by the harsh reality of it.

I place the papers in two piles, one for Katharine's letters and one for Laura's—mine. I place the already-read letters face down next to Katharine's pile. I decide to read the group of letters from my pile that coincides with what I have read from Katharine. After that, I will read one letter at a time from each pile to keep some sense of chronology. Many of them are dated; some are not, so far. I've left the photographs in a pile all by themselves waiting to be re-viewed, re-contextualized, and re-lived. I lean my back against a pillow supported by the end of the bed. Cross-legged on the floor I sit—a child contemplating a puzzle.

september 24, 1963
home economics

dear laura wells,
i saw what you were trying to do, but since you admitted it, are in corrective p.e. with me, and wear braces also . . . all right.

you are very lucky that your mother sews for you. i slaved over my skirt. my mother does not help me at all. i can't have sugar by the way. it makes my face break out. i am 13 going on 14.

friends maybe,
katharine isabel taylor

november 22, 1963
english class

dear laura,
    miss pointer stood up in front of the class and announced that john kennedy had been shot. i started crying. daryl (sits in the front row) turned around and said. "why is she crying?"
    how could he say that? darcy came up to me after and said she didn't blame me. she was crying too. in the hall many people were crying. i still am.
    kitty

march 18, 1964

dear laura,
    mother says you may spend the night during easter vacation. want to? you could probably walk over to our apartment and i'll meet you half way. we won't be able to stay up as late as we did at your house. my parents have

rules. lights out at 10. no noise since we live in an apartment. stuff like that. my dad has to watch his news programs all the time, nevermind that he falls asleep on the sofa.

your mother is so nice. where is her accent from? lucky that she's at work so much and you can do what you want. your grandmother is sweet. how sad that she talks to herself so much. it must be scary when she wanders off and you have to go looking for her. all my grandparents are dead. where did you say your father lived?

love, kitty

september 27, 1965
homeroom

dear laura,

i'm sorry i had to hang up, but my parents say that they do not want me tying up the phone line talking to you every night. they understand now that we are in different high schools and don't live near each other any more that we want to stay best friends. but mom said it's a toll call from the valley to hollywood. so we should keep writing back and forth. she said someday we will be glad we did. so i'll keep writing, if you will?

dad still does not have a job. and he comes home later and later from that bar he hangs out at, then he and mom fight.

now i'm awake and can't go back to sleep because mom is crying and i hear.

"no. larry i won't. leave me alone. i said no!" then i hear dad making those disgusting grunting noises.

i stay in my room with the door shut a lot. i'll be taking the bus to your house after school friday like always. i live for the weekends at your place. laura, i get my driver's license next month and i can't wait.

love, kitty

june 2, 1966
library

dear laura,

it's after school and i'm in the library again: anything to avoid going home and finding dad asleep in the green chair, in front of the tv. he's had four or more beers by then and . . .the chair is covered with cigarette burns. i can't take being around him and—sometimes . . . he . . . oh, i wish mom would leave him, but she won't . . . nevermind.

after my homework's finished, i walk to dutton's book store. i love the smell of books floor to ceiling. i get so involved that i have to rush to beat mom home at 5:30 p.m. i've finished hawaii by james michener. you'll love this book. it is a fat paperback, but worth reading. those poor hawaiians, how they suffered under the missionaries. you can borrow my copy. i've already started re-reading the group by mary mccarthy. (remember . . . it's about those eight vassar college graduates and their different lives that you liked so much?)

i felt like we were in college that afternoon we went to lunch at "room at the top" for my birthday. i love playing our fantasy game getting all dressed up in our suits and hats, pretending we're from millionaire families, traveling all over the world, living the jet-set life—while staring out at those panoramic views from sunset and vine.

i'm sorry i started to crack up when the waiter asked us if we wanted cocktails. you are better at that part of pretending than i am. he probably would have served us. but i was really nervous that we'd get caught.

see you at the dance friday. i'm wearing my white wide-lapeled suit with the pastel green little flowers on it. my hair gets a blunt cut tomorrow after school. dad's letting me drive the mustang, but i have to go home right after. no spending the night this time. drag, but i can take you home after the dance.

love, kitty

june 4, 1966
in my room

dear laura,

for english am supposed to be reading the scarlet letter. i am grounded for 2 whole weeks!! no spending the weekends at your house. dad got into the car in the morning and asked me why the seat was pushed back so far? it isn't worth it. i just told him straight out that sam drove. "well," he said "that's it then." that is all he ever says about everything. then he sits in his chair, turns the tv back on and drinks and drinks. oh god i hate this.

missing you already, kitty

July 14, 1989
Vista del Mar Inn
Santa Barbara
8:35 p.m.

Truth is seventeen-year-old Sam Chase drove us—me to my home and Katharine to hers. We rehearsed a fake scenario in case her dad caught on. Katharine would tell her dad that she and Sam were so involved talking in the car that I just pushed her over, started the car and drove her home while Sam's brother followed us in his car with his friends who took me home later after dropping Katharine off. Her dad wouldn't be as angry if he thought I had driven because her parents really liked me. Katharine was supposed to erase any possibility of a clue that someone else had driven the Mustang. She was to make sure the seat was pulled forward and that the ashtray only contained butts from her dad's cigarettes, Pall Malls, but she was too honest to do a thorough job of lying.

Sam and Katharine were stuck together at the dance like they were poured out of the same womb. Sam smoked Shermans. Katharine thought that gave him a risqué sense of being. He would read her passages from *Stranger in a Strange Land* by Robert Heinlein. Katharine wanted to "grok" Sam just like Valentine Michael Smith wanted to grok Romeo and Juliet. And Sam wanted to "grok" Katharine. That became a problem for a virginal sixteen-year-old like Katharine.

We both were committed to staying virgins through high school, or so we said. Most of the guys we knew or dated were committed to just the opposite. There was always this subtextual challenge when we dated. Should we . . . were we going to allow ourselves to be kissed goodnight on the first date? How soon before we allowed our dates to get to second base? A home run was something only a slut would do. To be called such a name was anathema to Katharine and me.

○

I stretch my legs and arms just like my cat Indy (born on Independence Day) does at home. I hear the pile of papers rustle and crinkle. I stand up and stretch some more. My neck hurts. I need some water, maybe even a brandy and a smoke. But all that comes to me is how I've watched Indy awaken from one of his many twelve-hour naps on our bed, pull his rump up high and bow his head down for that similar long low stretch and shudder that precedes his rush over to his bowl of Friskies. Then I let him outside to sniff the sunflowers in the garden where he puts his face right inside of them—never fewer than three—as if he were giving them a big morning hello kiss. How I miss his purring comfort just now. Raised by our neighbor, Hope, an elderly lady who owned beagles mostly, Indy loves to accommodate John when he points his mock-gun fingers at Indy and yells, "Bang!" Within seconds our thirty-pound tub of pumpkin orange with sherbet-pink nose and two little black dots in the center of his face rolls over and plays dead. This on his good-boy days when he is more orange than others, quite pleased with himself after catching a lizard—or a lizard's tail. When Hope died, her granddaughter asked us to keep nine-year-old Indy. We'd seen Indy do that hilarious trick many times, so jokester John gladly accepted him into our home.

I stand in my open doorway. The dark spreads its far-reaching veil onto the sand to the water's edge. The drab planked passageway paralleling the line of hotel rooms is dimly lit, and the moon is obscured a bit tonight. My growling stomach is drowned out by the crashing waves. The tide is up and the wind blows my silk robe slightly off of my right shoulder. God (*yawn*) I haven't bathed or changed in . . . too long. I exhale and turn back inside my room, ponder a shower and order a brandy and a burger instead. Hold the fries. Hold my head. Hold my life in this moment just for awhile. I need to relive another. I plop down on the carpet, smooth out the wrinkled papers, and continue.

○

11th Grade

Dear Kitty,
Study hall is borrrriinnnggg.
Tony picked me up Saturday night in his black 1957 T-Bird. His dad, an attorney for a bunch of entertainers, got us a front row box at the Hollywood Bowl. Saw Sergio Mendez and Brazil `66!!. Mais Que Nada, The Look of Love !! God it was cool!
Afterwards drove up to Mulholland to "check out the view" – kissing Tony gives my knees this rubbery kind of feeling. His kisses feel like purple velvet. Then, after making out for a few

minutes he slips his hand under my dress!! It actually felt kind of good when he rubbed my breast for a minute. Then, I heard Mom's voice going, "If you're not a virgin, a man won't have any respect for you!" so I pushed his hand away and said it was time to go home, because my curfew's still midnight and it was 11:30. This is the first time in the couple months since we've been dating that he's ever tried anything. Then he said that some of the girls at school say I'm this big flirt and that I fool around!! I told him that that was bullshit and that they're such liars—bitches all of them like Cathy, Avril, and Faline. So then Tony goes,

"Don't pay any attention to them they're just jealous because, you are one of the most bitchin' girls in school and they know it. I'd rather be with you any time." I was wearing my shocking pink mini-dress, the summery one that ties in a big bow in the back, my pink Mary Janes and matching clutch. Twiggy eyelashes painted on too.

Kitty, he is so <u>cuuute</u> with his blonde and neatly combed hair. I used to worry about bumping into his glasses when we kissed, but when we do I forget they're even there. He wants to go steady. God, can you believe it?! He is soooo popular.

Why does it always happen to me, Kitty, why are girls always talking behind my back—all the time? The minute I think I'm friends with one, I hear that she's stabbing me in the back. I think Faline really has a crush on Tony and she's jealous. That's what Mom says—that girls will always be jealous of me because I'm pretty and boys like me so much.

Sometimes, I wish we were ~~we were~~ living together all grown up in Paris or London with nothing to worry about and wealthy like in our fantasies. Thanks for being a true friend.

Love (I think I'm in love), Laura

○

Well into our junior year of high school, Katharine held onto her prized virginity, but unbeknownst to Katharine or anyone else I had already made my choice. His name was Alan.

Alan and I didn't consummate our relationship right away, we had to grow into it. I had a crush on him through most of our childhood. He was two years older and towheaded with sunburnt skin and azure eyes I wanted to swim in. In a family of Latinos he stood out like a Danish prince. The Danish was on his mother's side. The Mexican and French was on his father's side, my uncle Mike.

I lived for those Sundays when Mike brought Alan to visit our grandmother every other weekend. That was the visitation agreement between Alan's divorced parents. I lived in a house full of women owned by Grandma. We called her Mimi. It didn't matter why, we just did. So did my mom, her sister, and occasionally her sister's step-daughter—when she was home from boarding school.

When Alan came no one else mattered. The universe existed only for us—me with my long black pigtails and Alan with that hair that sparkled like pure crystal when the sunlight hit it. We'd go to the nearby playground driven by Uncle Mike in his old beat-up '56 DeSoto with push-button drive. Alan and I would swing on the swings together, play handball, hang from the bars and climb the jungle gym until we had to struggle for breath. When Alan left to go back to his mother's, I felt the sun exit from my life.

When Alan was 17 he ran away from his mom and her alcoholism, choosing to live with his father. Now I could visit Alan easily instead of waiting for him to visit me. The trick was convincing my mom to take the time to drive me. I prayed I'd turn sixteen on my next birthday instead of fifteen so I could drive myself, but it didn't happen. Fifteen did.

Alan and Mike lived a block from the beach in Redondo. We lived in the middle of Hollywood, just south of Hollywood Boulevard and east of Vine Street. It took almost an hour to get to Alan's place. There was no direct freeway route. Mom was too busy running her restaurant or too busy running somewhere more important than to take time out to drive me to see the one person I wanted to be near 24 hours a day. The one person I would have done 100 hula hoops for, when he was nine and I was seven, or later the one person I would give my body to without reservation. He already had my heart. So I waited.

The anticipated weekend came shortly after my fifteenth birthday. Mom's gift to me was a ride home with Uncle Mike after he worked one day for Mom baking bread in her small restaurant. Finally, I could spend time with Alan on his turf—the sea, surfboards, independence, smoking legal cigarettes—and illegal ones.

I soon discovered that Alan was allowed the kind of freedom I only fantasized about. He and his friends spent all their time on the beach surfing, partying, watching the sun rise and set, and somehow managing to go to high school in-between. Uncle Mike spent this weekend at his new girlfriend's house. Alan and I were on our own.

Their apartment was a one-bedroom, one-bathroom space with a tiny kitchen and dining area. In the meager living room was Alan's bed (a twin bed with the American flag as a bedspread), lengthwise against the wall by the hall to the bathroom and Mike's bedroom. Everywhere there were surfboards with names like Weber, Jacob, Hobie, and Con. Down on the floor, leaning against the far living room wall, behind the sofa and underneath the nicked mahogany coffee table, I counted six. The skegs on the board's tails made them all look like sharks lying in wait. There were two more in Mike's closet. He liked to bodysurf and had tried to teach me as a child, but I was never successful. I preferred jumping up and down in the water and dunking myself underneath the waves when they became too menacing.

Alan and I had gone to a party given by Bill Jergens, one of Alan's many friends from high school. At 16 Bill was already six feet tall, with albino white hair. His parents just happened to be away for the weekend. There was lots of alcohol, a little marijuana, and lots of smoking—Marlboro red-and-white hard packs, soft packs were a drag. Alex and Jean, 15 and 16, took hits off a joint they'd rolled. It was yellow and as big as a cigar, and the smoke blended with the Marlboros so you couldn't tell the difference between the grass and the cigarette smoke. There were three other girls who, unlike me, were yellow-haired, tanned, and blue and green eyed. Alan called them surf bunnies or "the chicks." I wondered if they were still virgins too? I was dark-skinned from Mom's side of the family, with black hair and brown eyes. I felt apart from this group who worshipped the ocean and wore shorts called Baggies with horizontal bands of bright color and button-down Hawaiian shirts with the tails hanging out or pull-over shirts with a stitched-on logo of little feet the guys called Hang Ten. And zinc oxide always still on their noses from surfing earlier in the day.

Alan introduced me announcing, "Hey everybody, this is my cousin from Hollywood, be cool. She's bitchin' okay?" He pushed at the air with his right hand to make sure everyone noticed.

Everybody did treat me "cool." The guys were either stoned or drunk, some were passed out on the floor or the sofa, some even snored. While the Beach Boys sang *Help Me Rhonda* on the radio, Jean and Alex started throwing up. I nursed them with cold facecloths on the backs of their necks, holding barf bowls I'd grabbed from the kitchen china. They were painted in a flower pattern in colors of purple, rust, and yellow. Almost too delicate for such a purpose, but they were all I could find.

The girls were curious about where I went to high school, then became disinterested after a few minutes. I guess coming from

Hollywood High seemed a bit too distant, too superficial from the earthiness of beach-loving life.

Most of the talk was about how stoked Bill was about a hot curl he'd shot at sunrise that day doing the dawn patrol. I looked down at his feet and noticed that all the shoes of choice were either thongs that displayed a multitude of surfing knots or faded black Converse tennis shoes. Then I looked at my Mandel's tan leather sandals purchased on Hollywood Boulevard. They looked a little too showy suddenly, with their gold buckles and prominent white stitched laces criss-crossing past my ankles.

Alan and I walked home the five blocks to his apartment, around 2 o'clock in the morning, both of us giggling. Alan from too much vodka and orange juice, me from rum and Coke. I only drank one drink. I never liked alcohol. Alan had lost count after four drinks and more joints. I was too busy playing nursemaid—and smoking marijuana just didn't do it for me (at least not yet). Thank God I had Alan's key because he started pounding on the door, forgetting he'd given it to me to hold for him in case he was too drunk to remember it.

We stumbled into the apartment and he fell straight onto the floor. He lay there moaning, his face now flushed red. I thought, Oh no, not another session with the barf bowl. But he slowly raised himself and collapsed on the bed struggling to remove his turquoise striped shirt. It brought out the color of his eyes, although they were quite bloodshot. I went into the bathroom and found a washcloth and ran it under the cold water faucet. I sat down beside him on the bed. He'd managed to remove his clothes, with the exception of his boxer shorts. I stared at the beauty of his glowing burnt-orange skin. His arms and legs were muscular, but not in a gross way. It was as if a sculptor had known exactly how much clay to remove, leaving just enough for definition of the limbs and firmness of the torso when creating this body of a perfect man within a seventeen-year-old boy.

I placed the wet cloth on Alan's forehead, trying to rub away the heaviness of too much drink and smoke from his reddened face, getting it to lighten to a peach-colored blush. He opened those pools of blue and looked at me. He gently put his hand on my shoulder.

"Thank you, thanks, Laura," he whispered.

I kept wiping his face, kept staring into his eyes, kept wondering what it would be like to kiss those slightly parted, wide lips of this boy I loved so much. He pulled me softly toward his mouth. We touched for a moment. There was heat, a white heat from him that pulled me further into that face that smelled of Russian Leather and Coppertone, into that body that welcomed me with a tenderness I'd only hoped for. My bikini top came off and I didn't know who or how, I only knew that he was sucking the desire from my breasts into his mouth and I wanted him to have me any way he wanted. I wanted him. I didn't care or wonder if this first time was right or wrong. I had only read about passion, not experienced it. I wanted Alan's passion for the ocean to engulf me. I felt such a craving for his kind of wave that I never wanted his body to stop from sweeping me away with it.

"Shouldn't we stop, do you want me to stop?" he asked between drowning me with French kisses and breathing more white heat into my ears and onto my neck. I answered by copying everything Alan did to me, doing it back to him. He led me and I willingly followed. I wanted to learn and I did, crying out when he penetrated my body. It hurt a little, but I felt more pleasure, a sort of ecstasy from the pain—pain that I had read about in books and talked about with other girls and thought I would hate and fear. I was a captive underneath him and that's where I belonged in that moment, in that crazy moment of abandoning all that was proper and sound. He held me in his own golden embrace and we slept, intent on holding fast.

We never talked about what happened, we just didn't see each other as often after that. School, working, living and loving others got in the way. This was not a share-secret, this was a—just-for-us . . . for me.

The year Alan dropped out of college he was in a car accident, the night before he was supposed to leave for basic training while driving Bill's British racing green convertible MG, too fast probably. They were both thrown from the car as Alan swerved to miss hitting a truck on Pacific Coast Highway at 1 o'clock in the morning. Seat belts were not required then. Bill lived. Alan didn't, his neck was broken.

At the funeral, I looked at Alan's face again, now cold like a wax work, dressed in a suit that wasn't his, with hair Brylcreamed back, almost straightening his natural wave. This was not the boy that four years earlier I had loved with all of my fifteen-year-old being. No, that boy was bathed in an auric light which was now beyond this stark physical empty shell of a body. Alan's essence, the part of his spirit that remained, was within *me*. It always would be, and no one would ever know.

○

I locate a 5x7 of Alan taken during a hiking trip. He wears blue jeans, suede hiking boots, a green long-sleeved woolen button-down shirt. Under those gentle hands with long adept fingers, Alan holds two bulky down jackets across his lap. I don't know whom the other one belongs to. Uncle Mike gave all of us in the family a copy of this photograph after Alan's death. I couldn't look at it then and I can barely look at it now—his loss remains a chasm in my life almost two decades later. Alan's flaxen hair looks scruffy and windblown. He sits on a large boulder on a rocky hillside half-smiling at the camera and squinting from the direct sunlight. Alan's face, that sunburnt, nose-peeling surf-washed face. I look for it even today in the faces of the young men I pass on the street, in the park, while jogging on the beach, or while walking in the sand at dusk. My early searches guided me to others, but never quite to that face, never quite that ocean-water smell, or salt-lick taste of drowning-in-sodium sun and foam atop waves ridden at dawn, long before the start of school.

But I'm getting ahead of myself. I put the picture down underneath the others. I light a Marlboro, white hard pack. Soft packs are still a drag.

I continued to let go of my teenage scruples in other ways, siding against my mother in anything I could. Ultimately trying drugs was a good way to assert my independence—or so I thought.

12th grade almost
Your eyes only Your eyes only Your eyes only Your eyes only Your eyes only

Dear Kitty,
Swear you won't say anything...........okay! The double date went like this:
Brenda and I smoked grass (you know, Brenda that works in Mom's restaurant after school)!! Her brother Eddie and his friend Rick turned us on. We parked in Rick's van down at Santa Monica Beach and smoked these huge, fat, yellow joints. The guys rolled them before they picked us up. Brenda and I were so nervous, but Eddie is a really cool guy, a senior, and he drives the

van for Mom's business delivering take-out orders.

When Brenda told me Eddie tried pot six months ago and that it was a really mind-altering experience, I said I was finally curious to try it too—soooo was she. Plus remember how Sam tried it and said it increases your perception of things. He let me borrow his copy of The Hobbit by J.R.R. Tolkien so I could read it after I get high. He says that marijuana is mentioned in there as pipeweed. Sam looks so cool smoking his Sherman cigarettes that I've decided I'm going to smoke them too. They make me cough, but I'll get used to them, I swear.

Grass feels a lot like drinking alcohol, but it doesn't make you sick like drinking does. Only, poor Eddie did end up getting sick and barfed all over the back of Rick's van. We had to go to a gas station and hose out the inside of the van.

When we took our first couple hits, it burned going down our throats, and the guys told us to hold it in for a couple seconds. Brenda and I were coughing real hard. Then after a while it didn't burn anymore. We started giggling cause everything seemed so funny. The four of us walked on the beach for a while and I could feel the wind blowing against my skin like chiffon wrapping itself around my body.

Kitty, we absolutely, positively <u>haaave</u> to try this together, I know you said it's not your thing, but it would be such a trip.

Love ya,
Laura

Mrs. Susan Wells
cordially invites you to attend a
Sweet Sixteen Party
in honor of her daughter
Laura Mimi
on Sunday, April 23rd, at 12:00 noon

Pike's Verdugo Oaks
1010 North Glendale Avenue
Glendale, California

R.S.V.P HO 5-2945 or TR 2-7070

april 24, 1967
HAPPY BIRTHDAY

dear laura,

this card is simple; the phrase is simple; but the thought is not. at last you have arrived at your 16th year! may it be wild and groovy! hope you begin to find yourself and answer your puzzling questions. live this 16th year for me cause i seemed to have lost it. may your eyes always shine with happiness and not tears. be good and keep smiling,

love always, kitty

September 2, 1967

dear laura,

it is going to be hard to get back into school. staying at your house on the weekends is the only way i can survive.

dad still gets up late and stares at that stupid television all day. when mom gets home they have drinks. she cooks dinner. and then he goes out to one of his stupid bars. i don't talk to him anymore. mom refuses to drive the car at all. it makes her nervous. she still takes the bus to work. i dread coming home. he makes me . . . . nevermind.

going to the whiskey every weekend for all of july and august and dancing to pierre's band gave me such a feeling of freedom. did you know all the boys in the band went to elementary school together with sam?

he says pierre is a drop-out and wants to go into rock and roll seriously. i saw the two of you looking pretty stoned when you came back from your "walk" on the strip. sunset strip: all those hippies, druggies and far-out looking people. i love watching them.

sam wanted me to smoke with him. but it does nothing for me. i explained to him why and how even the smell of my parents' cigarettes in our apartment makes me ill.

you don't realize how lucky you are that your mom lets us stay out until 4:00 in the morning. mom still doesn't know that we get in that late. we aren't doing anything wrong. i mean . . . dance until 2:00 a.m, go to breakfast at the pancake house and home. since when does time of day have anything to do with getting into trouble? should we count the two hours we spend in your bathroom putting on makeup?

senior year is ahead. feels like we're ten years older than we are.

○

Twenty-four sixteen-year-old girls, makeup methodically applied, lips adroitly frosted, shiny eyeliner painted on along with a layer or two of false eyelashes coiffed and cologned, sat around four tables of six singing Happy Birthday to me. Most of them—with the exception of Kitty, my family, and some who went to different schools—didn't really like me. My Hollywood High classmates—the student council stuck-ups and suck-ups, and rich girls, or those who liked boys who liked me instead—didn't really like me at all. I knew it, that's why I invited them just to see who would come. Surprisingly, most of them showed up.

They made fun of my low-cut baby-blue-jersey mini-dress. My cups "runneth-ed" over and in the elegant floor-to-ceiling mirrored bathroom one of the cliques spitefully prattled on about them while Brenda, a friend and my mole, listened from a stall nearby. Truth was Mom was just too worn-out to adjust the Jean Patou pattern for my C cups. She only had time to sew late at night after a long day at work, her eyes too tired to see clearly. She tailored the pattern designed for a flat-chested wraith as all the models in the photos were then. I was a wraith— but not my blooming boobs.

I see shoes, my shoes, and two other pairs attached to long legs in the bottom of a black-and-white photo as I lean over toward the coffee table at an odd angle to put out my third cigarette in a row. I quit so long ago, but can't get enough of them now, damn it. I will quit when I get home, I promise, I promise, so help me. I scoop up the 8x10 glossy circa-end-of-1967 taken some eight months after my Sweet Sixteen. Holding this photograph of myself and two of my dearest girlfriends during the last of our high school years, I gulp the little last bit of brandy; it goes down hard. So does this memory.

○

The three of us pose side by side in the old photo. The best of friends facing the camera lens in front of Mother's white French provincial breakfront in the entryway of our 1920s bungalow-style two-bedroom, one-bath home, southeast of Hollywood and Vine. Brenda stands between Kitty and me. At sixteen years old, I'm almost a full year or two younger than they are. At 10 o'clock at night, New Year's Eve is closing in on us. We have been crowded together in my bathroom for more than two and a half hours, applying just the right amount of lipstick, eyeshadow, blush, hair pins and hair spray. None of us girls has a date. We are dressed for a night of dancing and club-hopping on the Sunset Strip. Gazzari's. The Whiskey. I am sad. My boyfriend, Pierre, a seventeen-year-old bass player in my favorite band, The Abstracts, broke up with me a few months earlier. I am now invisible to him. He only has eyes for another girl, Andy, who also follows his band around from club to club.

Tonight he will not notice me while his band plays. He will not see me while I dance and try to attract his eye. We three friends just have each other and will join some of the other guys we hang around with, who don't have real dates either, and share a kiss or two or three after midnight.

Even though it is difficult to tell in this photo, Brenda and Kitty are light-skinned natural blondes with aquamarine blue eyes. Each of them looks like a typical blonde, blue-eyed surfer girl, the kind the Beach Boys sing about in their famous Top Ten song "California Girls." I, with my olive skin, black hair, and brown eyes, do not. Brenda and I wear mini-dresses a full seven or eight inches above the knee. Kitty wears a chiffon pants suit. We all appear to be wearing white, but we're not, except for Brenda. Kitty wears pink and orange paisley. I wear silver mesh over silver fabric. Mom has spent several days, late at night after work, sewing this dress from a Rudy Gernreich Vogue pattern. Mom also sewed Brenda's white wool dress with white-and-yellow daisy trim from a Vogue pattern. We're all wearing our Mary Jane squash heels. We have ever so delicately glued on our two layers of false eyelashes. We have carefully painted Twiggy liner, stroke by deliberate stroke, underneath our eyes. My uncle Bernie positions us, counts to three, and says "Hold it!" so each of our moms will have a record of their three young nubiles. Seniors, all in high school. So sure of ourselves. So young. So refreshingly naive. This before the clock strikes twelve, aging us, moving us out into life on our own terms. Unfortunately, Kitty's eyes blink shut.

I marvel at how good her eye makeup looks, probably because of the full hour I spent applying it. Bernie cannot do a retake. He's run out of film. This will be his last shot. This will be the last time the three of us ever stand together in just this way. Joined for this flash of an instant before scattering out into the night, into our lives.

One month later the Tet offensive will begin; during traditional January holidays, the North Vietnamese will attack more than thirty major South Vietnamese cities and towns, catching the American military off-guard.

Four months later, on a spring day in Tennessee, while visiting Memphis in support of a 1968 sanitation workers' strike, Martin Luther King will be killed on the balcony of the Lorraine Motel by a sniper's bullet.

Five months away, high school graduation awaits, after which most of the guys I march down the aisles into the Hollywood Bowl with, keeping pace to the sound of "Pomp and Circumstance," will report to the draft board in downtown Los Angeles. Many will later be classified 1A and sent to fight in Vietnam. Most will return forever changed. Some will not return at all. Others will draft-dodge straight to Canada or stay and march in protest against this so-called police action.

Six months away, shortly after midnight on June 5, Bobby Kennedy will speak to his followers while campaigning for the presidency in the nearby Ambassador Hotel. As he leaves through the kitchen he will be killed by an assassin's bullet. Nearly a year away is the Democratic Convention in Chicago, which escalates into a full-blown teargas-the-hippie-protesters-against-the-war riot. The three of us will cry, not standing together just in this way, but sitting in our homes, talking on the phone, watching the chaos on television.

Sweet 16 was never sweet. I was not innocent and had been quite a bit more than kissed. So had Kitty, but I didn't know it then. What else didn't I know? Or should I be asking myself what else I didn't *want* to know?

Chapter Three:
Awakenings

July 15, 1989
Vista del Mar Inn
Santa Barbara
4:54 a.m.

That noise. Stop. Stop that ringing. I don't want to wake up yet . . . I'm at the beach, the surf is . . . is . . . wet. *Shit.* That's spilled—God . . . that fucking phone.

"Hello." My tongue is stuck to the roof of my morning mouth.

"So, you don't really care, do you?"

"Huh . . . Mom! is that—"

"I don't know who's supposed to be here today, and I am *all alone.*"

"Mom, where's Ana?"

"I don't need her. You tell everyone I'm stupid and blind. You don't care a damn about me."

"Mom—"

"*Hay dios mío*, why am I still here? I ask you. I ask God to take me and he's forgotten my address—"

"Mom—"

"*Mija*, when are you coming to see me? You never come to see me. What have I done to you? You never understood me. You never liked me. You treat me like I'm a servant or worse a slave. Why, God, why am I still alive? I ask him, why God why. Where are you? What are you doing, *mija?*"

"Mom, put Ana on the phone."

"Ana, OYE . . . *muchacha* . . . *muchacha* . . . Ana." I should be asking God, why God, why? Damn it John, why did you have to give her my number? Ana says that Mom woke up at 3 o'clock in the morning all ready to go to church. Ana had to calm her down and remind her that the church services are tomorrow at 10 o'clock. Ana says she'll try to explain where I am and why. I promise to call back later.

Need a shower. Coffee spilled all over the bed. I roll over on a letter. Smells like chocolate. I used to have a special pen in high school that wrote in brown ink and tasted of chocolate. Kitty gave it to me just prior to high school graduation. I'd die for chocolate. After graduation, Kitty was dying to get away from her parents. Afraid of dying in Vietnam, so many of our high school friends overwhelmed by the draft threatening to transport them to the land of rains, hovering mists, and intolerable sock-rotting-in-combat-boots-heat, continued spending endless marijuana obsessed hours figuring out more ways to avoid the draft. I was too busy medicating myself with illegal drugs to notice their fear, or Kitty's pain and my own.

I pull the slept-on letter out from under me, careful not to tear an edge. Just a glance before that shower, just a quick look. Where are my cigarettes?

While I take a hit and blow it out, I am carried by the things I want to read, want to remember, *should* remember. Memory enslaves me like a drug. It commands that I forget what I want to remember and retain what I want to forget. I will take from it what I must . . . what I need.

12th grade Graduation Week!!

Dear Kitty,
Another week and we're out of these dumps, for real. THANK GOD!! Freedom from this bullshit. At lunch yesterday, a bunch of us were sitting on the Sunset lawn and I could see some kids next to us passing ~~Seconals~~ reds around.

Everybody's so freaked with Vietnam. Some of the guys in ROTC have volunteered to go after graduation—real dorks! But most of Tony's friends are either splitting to Canada or their parents are hiring attorneys to get them out of the draft.

Somebody asked Lou Spindler at the dance last month whether he was going or not and he goes,

"Not me man, I don't like rice patties." He was really wasted. Now I hear he's classified 1A and going. I think the whole thing is one big bummer.

Hey, was that a trip at Diane's house last weekend. Can you believe what she said about her and Jonathan. She's only 17 and sending him nude pictures of herself! God, I swear, she looked like an older woman in her 20's in those photos. I can understand him being in Vietnam and missing her, but do you believe what she said about—what did she call it—"going down on him" and then when she said,

"Go ahead ask your moms, they'll tell you." How come she was so sure? I can't picture my parents doing that to each other no matter what she says. Swallowing some guy's—YUUUCH!!! Do you think, maybe, it's because she's black and just black people do that? Or because she's going to be a professional dancer and has more experience from all those auditions? You're right let's not grow up.

Brenda, Darcy and I are going to park on Mulholland and smoke a couple joints together before driving to the Hollywood Bowl. If we have to sit there for a couple hours during graduation, we might as well.

Peace and love,
Laura

november 7, 1968

dear laura,

where have you been for the last three days? you haven't been in any of our classes! darcy says she doesn't know where you are. we both think you and gil are together somewhere. we've got tests in sociology and english coming up. remember, if you miss more than three classes you're dropped. since you and your mom haven't been getting along, i didn't want to call.

i'm sorry, but i can't hack hanging out on sunset strip as much as you do. the drug thing scares me. remember why i broke up with sam? i'm so worried about you! you're taking a big chance carrying a lid of grass around in your purse during school. i know you said "no sweat, things are so laid back in college. god, we can even smoke in class!" but i'm afraid you're going to get busted.

love, kitty

12/68
Never fucking never winter wonderland

Dear Kitty,

I'm sick as shit with the flu, and grounded from using the phone. Busted is the right word. Mom threw me in Juvey!!

I didn't come home Saturday night because I was with Gil at somebody's crash pad where a group of us walked from The Whiskey to get high. Shane was in the bedroom screwing that platinum bleached hooker we see hanging around all the time. So, dig this, she has her period and we spy Shane doing a Pink Panther sneak out around 4 a.m. to dump a bundle of sheets in the trash. It was a crack-up! There was no place for Gil and I to fool around so we just crashed on the floor next to some of the other bodies. I got home around 3 o'clock the next day. Mom had left for work, so I went to work. Lion in Winter is still playing and after I seat people I like to stand in the back and watch it. I've seen it at least 50 times. Peter O'Toole and Katharine Hepburn are so-together.

Anyhow, Mom shows up around 10:00 p.m. to pick me up. I know I'm up shit's creek, because she never leaves the restaurant before midnight on the weekends. I usually take the bus home, right?

"I told you if you spent another night away from the house with that worthless son-of-his-mother that would be IT. You're going downtown to talk to a policeman." She doesn't say another word the rest of the ride.

So then I'm talking to Sergeant so and so with a hick accent, who starts asking me all these questions about how many times I toke up each day. What the hell does toke up mean? I was honest with the guy, because Mom wasn't in the room. He figured I'd smoked around 200 joints over the last three months. I never counted before, God, it sounded like I was an addict or something?! Then he puts me in this room with one window, closed Venetian blinds and a table. So I turn out the bright lights and crash on top of it. It was so weird because the Sergeant locks me in. Next thing I know I'm on my way to Central Juvenile Hall with two pigs driving 90 miles an hour and I'm getting thrown all over the back seat into the lap of the cop next to me. By the time I get to this place it's 2 a.m. and some half-asleep woman makes me take off everything and give it to her. They give me this crummy blue thing to sleep in and I'm locked into a cell with a bed, a toilet, and a sink.

Next morning I'm put into a ward with a bunch of other girls. All of them, close to my age, and looking pretty harmless, right? The youngest was 9 yrs. old and in on a prostitution charge. The big question everybody has for each other is:

"So, what are you in for?"

"Being incorrigible," I answer.

"Huh, no way man, you can't be in here for just that, you musta done somethin' else," goes this Mexican 15-year-old chick with big boobs and sweaty arm pits. "You sure you dindo somthin' else like runninway?"

"Uh, yeah maybe—I didn't come home for a day." I figure that counts.

"No, no way that's not enough of a reason, girl, you gotta begone forleas 3 days or more. I know man, I been here 5 times since I was 10."

Then it hits me; good old Mom doing her let's-teach-Laura-a-lesson-bullshit probably insisted to the cops I stay here. This place is not going to beat me. Boredom here gets everybody crazed. So I volunteer for any clean up—something I've had lots of practice at. Scrubbing toilets, floors and walls, for 3 wonderful days. Just like cleaning up Mimi with her accidents at home.

My last night 50 of us are sleeping on mattresses on the floor and somebody starts crying, then everybody in the whole room starts wailing. All of us tough girls, we're all crying. Crying for our Mommies, our anybodies, ourselves.

Out on six months probation, I'll be 18 in five, knowing I'm not going to quit doing drugs, no way. I'll just be a lot more careful, play the game, straighten up and get a full-time job so I can get the fuck out of this house.

Want to be my roommate? Flunking all of my classes so I'm dropping out of college. No one is ever going to take my freedom away from me again. No one.

Love, your favorite ex-con,

Laura

Vista del Mar Inn
Santa Barbara
July 15, 1989
8:03 a.m.

Walked on the beach, in front of the hotel, at sunrise. Watched the cherry and orange sun do a lollipop rise from behind the mountains illuminating the sky, the water, my brain. I felt Katharine's presence and her footsteps in the sand next to mine. Reading over our words of 26 years ago is like peeking into the brain matter of the characters in one my stories. I'm rediscovering strangers. *That* Laura was not real, just someone I made up, wasn't she? A confused and misguided kid. Katharine was so in-control and adult at such a young age. When did we switch roles?

At 17, I remember sitting in Mom's purple Chevy Impala, parked in the Mayfair market parking lot on the corner of Fountain and La Brea Avenues. Mom was sobbing as I "confessed" to giving away my virginity (Alan was never mentioned) on New Year's Eve, two weeks before. A great way to ring in 1969, I said. But it wasn't supposed to happen that way, she cried, not to her little girl. Juvenile Hall was just before that.

"You should have waited, Laura, for an older man (*sob*) with more experience (*sob, sob*), not some stupid kid who knows nothing (*sob, sob, sob*)!" That's how it happened to Mom. At seventeen. Older man. Or so she told me once. A black-and-white photograph that hangs in our home is the living proof of the act. In it Mom wears an exquisitely embroidered Spanish mantilla. It's now draped in all its flaming silk red, green, blue, and cream over our baby grand piano in the living room. In the photograph, Mom stands in front of a full-length mirror with the mantilla wrapped around her bare and supple tiny body. She has turned to face the camera as if beckoned quickly to do so. Her lustrous black wavy hair hangs down to her knees. Exotic and wicked, she smiles. She knows. His name was Emory, 45. He owned a car dealership on Hollywood Boulevard. He was very wealthy and loved dressing her in seductive clothes—his little exotic and fiery doll saronged in a mantilla. I can only imagine that behind the camera he is smiling knowingly too. It didn't last. The following year, 1929, the economy imploded and that was hard on everyone. Emory lost his car lot and his career and disappeared. Maybe the story was she left him, but afterward Mom went from conquest to conquest, or so she told me. But that is all forgotten now.

Her remembering depends upon where she is in the caverns of her mind on a particular day at a particular hour, moment, or second. It's as if she is walking on a street, lost, but then an alley pops up, and she has a vague recollection from twenty years before of a painted red doorway halfway down that alley she spies, and she thinks she might have even walked through that door, but then again, maybe she just passed by it, or perhaps someone she knew walked out of it and embraced her, and they might have even stood in front of that red door and talked for a time, but about what she is not sure, but again maybe they didn't, and she has confused that red door from the one on the street with another just around the corner and maybe she just needs to take a quick run over there and see if that red doorway is really there, but then she forgets where she is, and why she is there suddenly, and on and on andonandonandonandon. The memory of her life once lived keeps slipping through her fingers; the more she struggles to hold on to it, the more it dissipates, then evaporates, and she's left mute. Until she calls me, of course.

The thing, too, about memory is that it's all about subtracting and adding. 1989 -78=1911, the year of Mom's birth, although she prefers to say that she is ten years younger and was born in 1921. But that would mean that she lost her virginity at six or seven years of age, I remind her.

"But that's right," she says.

"Mom, that's impossible," I insist. She insists that I don't know how to add and changes the subject five times in the span of four minutes.

1989 - 40=1949, the year of Katharine's birth. She died in her fortieth year, but didn't turn 40 until three months after her death; so was she technically 39. Or 40?

1951 + 17=1968, the year I lost my virginity, according to Mom's memory, but really it was two years earlier, so 1951 + 15= 1966. So which one really counts? Mom has no memory of 1966. But the version I told her happened in 1969, or at least I said it did. And Mom has no memory of that either, depending upon which intersection between *was* and *is* she stands on.

Another thing about memory is that it can contradict the truth, and so sometimes lies are necessary to find the truth. Or are they?

Gil West, at 17, looked almost like he could have been Katharine's brother. He was six-foot-one, spoke with an English accent, had hair cut like Paul McCartney's, and he was a drug user—like me. Dancing with him at The Whiskey was sensuous, but sensuous had come long before.

○

I'm lying on top of Mom's double bed with the faded lavender chenille bedspread. I trace the flower patterns on the soft surface with my index finger. I've loved this spread since I was a little girl. When it's on Mom's bed I can't resist the urge, even at thirteen, to lie on it, curl up in a ball, and sleep in peace and safety.

I'm reading a very graphic sex scene in Mary McCarthy's book *The Group*. Kitty left it for me when she slept over this weekend. I'm feeling the same as the college girl in the book. I hunger for the arousal she hungers for, and I want the man to make love to me as she does. I feel like I could give myself to the first man I see. I don't know what to do. I feel such desire, is that the right word? My mouth feels dry and there is such a feeling down there—between my legs. I put a pillow between them and squeeze my knees tightly around it. One of our new kitties is licking my arm. He is a white furry little thing.

I place him on top of my chest where my nightgown falls open and he begins to lick near my breast. It feels interesting. I lift up my nightgown and coax the little thing to lick further down my body; my hip, my thigh, my groin. He does, rapidly, as he is still a baby and not yet weaned. I place him close to my vagina and he licks and sucks me like he would his mama cat. I hear his suckling noises as my body experiences such waves of motion. I can feel the movement in my vagina and I'm terrified by it. The little one has run off, frightened by my gasping. Is this it—orgasm? I don't know, but I feel elated and exhausted. Who would have thunk it?

○

This response to my budding hormones has been locked away in a secret place that houses all unmentionable-and-better-forgotten-memories. I walked around for days, all those years ago, feeling acutely ashamed of my 13-year-old brush with bestiality. My innocent little victim ran away two days later.

When my day of breakage did occur, penetration with Alan was similarly satisfying, forbidden, yet bloodless. With Alan it had all been as if in a dream. It was a dream and I felt no stain because in my mind it was fantasy, too astonishing to be real. Too incestuous to admit.

With Gil, penetration was painful and anti-climactic. So much so that I could no longer deny admission to the Club of Womanhood and accepted that everyone who saw me would know. The little girl I really was, now was betrayed by that woman—by her walk, the swaying of her hips, the knowing smile on her face and the depth in her dark amber eyes.

The stain of not-quite-virgin blood on that white twin-bed sheet, wrapped around me in Gil's seedy apartment building in the middle of Hollywood, released me to cross over the border of curiosity and unknowing into knowing. Bounding across this threshold flamed a desire that wanted to consume the world. Katharine never bounded into anything, at first; she stepped gingerly, but stumbled all the same.

may 23. 1969
bates accounting corp.

dear laura.

i like your new apartment. you and darcy seem to get along well. i am still not sure of the results of the test, but will know monday. the thought of being.

well . . . eric doesn't care or want to know anything about it. he drove off and left me standing there when i told him. he hasn't come to psychology class since. it's over. this receptionist job in the accounting office is okay. it's a short bus ride from home. dad will let me take the car, he says, once in a while if i have to work late. it's slow right now and everyone is out to lunch. once school's out i'll be working here full-time. there are several elderly ladies working here. it's like being surrounded by grandmothers . . . i have not been able to sleep very well . . . phones ringing. must run.

"be of love (a little) more careful than anything else" e.e.cummings.
love always, kit

I forgot how much Katharine held herself in check. It took adulthood to share the true pain of living with alcoholic parents. She was unable to say "alcoholic." She was unable to talk in detail about her dead sister—a sister who was ten years older with two children of her own. When Katharine was ten, her 20 year-old sister, along with her 16-month-old baby girl and three-year-old son, died in a car accident. Betty, named after her mother, had made many poor choices in most of her short life. A rebellious and pregnant runaway who finally settled into a regular job, an apartment, and another disposable marriage, Betty had worked double shifts at her waitress job at the long-gone Cherry House coffee shop in Van Nuys, and then chose to drive north one Sunday morning to San Luis Obispo to the Men's Colony so that the little girl could visit her daddy, Betty's latest ex-husband, an immigrant from Guatemala, doing time for another round of burglaries. Betty didn't even want to go, but Carlos had pleaded with her to bring up his little daughter. Maybe Betty was tired, or maybe the road was slippery from a light rain as dawn was breaking, her parents were never sure. Betty's Karmann Ghia careened across the center of the 101 Freeway, flipping the car over onto the southbound side where it skidded off into a ditch upside-down. The baby and Mama died instantly. The three-year-old died on the way to the hospital. Katharine loved Bett, as she called her, but she wasn't around for most of Katharine's early years. When Bett did show up, it was only to be brought home by the police for some foolish teenage infraction, or to be locked in her room by her father for disappearing for days at time. Bett loved nothing more than to taunt the Taylors by flouting their futile discipline.

Katharine was the good girl, the did-everything-right girl who obeyed the rules, kept her room immaculate, and never argued with her parents. Bett hated everything about her parents and for Katharine, Bett was just a dense fog clouding and disrupting the family routine. And then just as Katharine felt like she was getting to know Bett (Katharine loved playing with her little niece and nephew that last morning she saw them), this catastrophe swamped the family like a tsunami, drowning everyone in grief, self-pity, and denial then numbness. Neither Bett nor her children were ever discussed in the Taylor household again. There were no photographs of any of them in their apartment, no mementoes of the lives of the three who had disappeared so suddenly from the Taylors' world. It was as if they never existed. Instead Larry Taylor just drank away the memories of his eldest daughter and grandchildren. And so for him they were a vague impression, a forced forgotten blur.

Betty Taylor smoked two packs a day, drank, and plunged herself into her career. Work was all that mattered to her. She was an executive secretary for the president of Security Pacific Bank in North Hollywood. It was demanding and her boss expected her to put in overtime all the time. Liquid lunches were not uncommon, but Betty senior could still function even on a "full tank." Taking on any extra project she was given, she was more than willing to do everything she was asked to do. After all, she typed 100 words a minute and took shorthand almost as fast. A "little" gin, as Betty claimed, didn't intrude on that skill, and someone had to pay the bills. Larry only worked enough to pay his bar tab, but when Katharine and I were growing up together, he could barely pay anything, so Betty just worked harder.

It was not until years later that Katharine told me that Bett had existed and how she died, speaking of it in hushed tones as if we were in a church instead of in her parents' apartment.

Katharine said she used to wait up, every night, for her father to arrive home from his boozing, no matter what hour. It was only then she could sleep, for just a few hours, before she had to wake for school. At first, Katharine thought her mother was to blame for Larry's nightly disappearances. Later, Katharine sided against her father, begging Betty to leave him. But the woman always refused.

Larry made Katharine uncomfortable, made me uncomfortable. Most of my girlfriends' fathers affected me like aliens from another planet. A "father" was a person I was not accustomed to being around.

My own father left when I was four and we never heard from him again. Mother said they fought all the time and made love all the time, but she was the one who made sure there was money in the bank and food on the table. After four years, Mom figured out it was easier to do all that without him. I like to think I was the product of fighting, forgiving, fucking and flight.

Larry Taylor had a brooding, dubious air about him, and it wasn't just his alcoholism. I never mentioned my dim opinion of her father to Katharine and could never completely put my finger on why he gave me such uneasiness every time I saw him.

The Taylors' drinking influenced Katharine in the opposite direction. If she wasn't sure who she wanted to be, she sure as hell knew who she *didn't* want to be. We'd get drunk at slumber parties with other girlfriends, but Katharine always stopped after one drink. She was so much the grown up in our relationship, watchful and worrisome. I, most decidedly, was none of those things.

Dear Kit,

"Thank God," I said, when I saw the note Darcy plastered on the wall in big letters, KIT IS NOT PREGNANT! No kidding, she writes it on a grocery bag and tapes it on the bedroom wall. She said you sounded a little upset even though you were glad about the news. I've been calling you, nobody's home. Your office says you're out sick, but they wouldn't say what was wrong??

Darcy and I have been dropping mescaline on the weekends. What a trip! It's mellower than acid. It's like smoking a heavy amount of dope and dropping a little bit of acid. We clean the apartment from top to bottom on Saturday mornings and then we sit back and take our tabs with Gatorade. Somebody told me it's supposed to get the stuff through your system faster. Anyway, we just sit around and groove on the apartment—the green carpet patterns start to lift off the floor and the posters all come alive off the walls. When I move my hands back and forth I can see traces of each individual hand movement. Darcy and I get so hung up staring at 20 or 30 hands suspended in the air. I love hallucinogenics!

Last week I ran into Shane and his friend Josh. I was waiting at the bus top to go home, across the street from work and Shane drives by in a foxy green Alfa Romeo convertible. I jumped in, we picked up Josh, and I brought them to the apartment and they stayed for the whole week! Josh was this really funny guy. We laughed a lot. I'd forgotten how handsome Shane is. Tall, dark hair, and a cool dresser; brown suede jackets and dark brown Fred Segal bell-bottoms. That's where he was when he spotted me. It's across the street from where I work.

We jammed into our pushed-together twin beds. <u>Ménage a quatre,</u> baby!

Thank God for birth control pills. Darcy and I take them at the same time, toasting our paper cups with wine.

Honestly though, we mostly rapped with the guys the whole night. All of us were just too wired to really do anything physical. We'd taken some very intense mescaline that one of the guys at work sold me. Stayed up for 36 hours straight before crashing. Still recovering. Slept for 12 straight hours after those guys left.

Hey, Kit, why don't you come and stay overnight? How come you haven't called? It has been too long—
Love ya,
Laura

7/69

Dear Mrs. Taylor,

After we hung up last night, I felt I had to write this note to you to let you know, again, how sorry I am about Katharine. I knew she was upset about things, I wish I had realized just how much. I'm sure placing her in Woodley Hospital was the only thing you could do.

I pray things will turn out okay. I love Kitty very much and is there anything I can do? I know you said she isn't supposed to have visitors or phone calls, but if that changes, please let me know.
Sincerely,
Laura Wells

august 7, 1969
woodley hospital

dear laura,

i go home at the end of the month. it feels like a year since i arrived. my "escape" made my stay here last longer. they told me they don't like their patients walking off from an outing to a movie theater. you were right to bring me back, but i thought they would punish me for being bad.

dr. peluso asked me why i wanted to be punished. i told him i needed to be. i'm not a nice girl. he said i should take two white pills every day and i would feel like a nice girl.

i don't want them.

don't you want to go home?, he said.

not home to my parents, i said.

time to move into your own place. make a life separate from them, he said.

they cannot afford to keep me here. it's too expensive, i said.

laura, what's out there for me?

"if a man does not keep pace with his companions perhaps it is because he hears a different drummer..."

thoreau

love, kit

9/69

Dear Kit,

My third and last date with Gaylord Ellis was such a bad scene. God, just because he's this famous science fiction writer and only 5' 3", he has to make up for his lack of height with a superiority complex. Remember that sci-fi movie that he wrote about that guy who talks to his pet bear cub. Then at the end when the bear cub is dying, the guy kills off his new wife and feeds her to the bear to save the dying bear! Now I know why.

Some of the other editors in the office (most of them homos) were taking bets he was going to get me into bed. I knew they'd all lose.

We're at Gaylord's house in Laurel Canyon, it's gorgeous with a toy room for grown-ups and I'm in there playing table hockey. We smoked some great weed (he always gets the best), but this time I'm feeling a bit paranoid. Then he calls to me from his bedroom and I walk in and he is standing there in nothing but his underwear by his bed which is up four steps on a pedestal, draped with a canopy of red velvet with a large gold crown on it. Does this guy have an ego or what!? I ran out of the house into my car and split!! Now when he comes into the office he won't speak to me anymore. Shine him on! Now I realized why he insisted on waiting till my 18th birthday before we started dating. So much for dating a 35-yr.-old. All the editors lost their bet...I won 50 bucks. Ha!

Love and Why Me?
Laura

december 15, 1969

dear laura,

yes, it is funny that we are seeing each other. all that time we were in school with joy chan and now, for me to be dating her older brother and living in this rented room. the people downstairs are very quiet and reserved so when lee stays over he has to climb out of the window and down the drain pipe.

why is it when he touches me i feel nothing?

it's so still up here in the early mornings. sometimes i sit in the corner and imagine myself small. the room and its contents grow larger and larger. i shrink into this tiny little insect. i can walk around the floor.

the grooves in the wood look like huge fissures. it takes me all day to reach the bed across the room. i can hide this way, laura, and no one can find me. not my parents, not lee, not even you.

i like not having a phone. when lee comes over late, he has to throw pebbles at my window.

i see mom for lunch once in a while. our offices are a short bus ride apart. i don't talk to my dad if i can help it. he's usually gone when i call--at one of his usual places.

"Reality proves very little and it indicates a great deal..." D. Berrigan
love always, kit

1/70

Dear Kit,

I quit work because I couldn't take the bullshit from the editor I work with on the magazine anymore. So we have this huge fight and she screams,

"Laura, why the fuck aren't you at your desk, I'm sick of looking for you all the God damned time," in front of everyone. I reminded the cunt that I was getting something she asked me to find and I say,

"That's it, I quit, Lacey," and I picked up my stuff and got the hell out of there, called Mom, told her I was giving up the apartment and moving home. I couldn't afford to stay there anymore (Darcy says she's ready to move home too and save some money for a nicer apartment next summer).

I still think Lacey has attitude because of that time she made a pass at me. Remember, I told you how I went to her house to pick up some hash brownies she'd made and she walks out of her bedroom stark naked. That's when I realized all the rumors about her being a dyke were true. God, was I freaked!

Anyway, after work that night Josh, Darcy, Shane and I went to the midnight showing of Woodstock. We'd all dropped different hallucinogenics. I tell Shane that I took a tab called Orange

Sunshine (one of the editors at work copped it for me) and he looks at me kind of freaky and says,

"Shit, that's a 4-way tab!"

I didn't know. Ralph, the guy who sold it to me, said it was a real trip. I figured, far-out.

So now my brain feels like it's on the tip of a rocket ship to the moon. I can't talk straight. My eyes feel like they're popping out of my head. Everything outside of the theater is breathing and moving at different speeds. The streets are pulsating. No. Rolling ocean waves, big ones. All cars are a blur, traffic lights are swaying and dancing the Watusi. I have visions of blowing my cool; flipping out crazy, hysterical, and raving. I see myself put into a straight jacket by orderlies, strapped onto a gurney and wheeled into an ambulance off to the funny farm; the ultimate bad trip. Suddenly Josh is saying,

"Laura, just maintain, ok, maintain, we're getting you out of here."

We split back to Shane's house, lucky he has his own entrance so we don't wake up his mom. Josh brews some marijuana tea and Shane dumps Seconals and 3-grain Tuinals on the table. Darcy passes around a joint. I try everything. Lots of everything.

My body slows down some, but when I open my mouth to talk, the words come out in slow motion. My head is ten sentences ahead of my mouth.

It's now 4 a.m. Darcy and I go home. She crashes. I can't, so I watch TV. After a while I realize the TV is not turned on, but I swear I'm watching The Twilight Zone where the guy kills his wife by pushing her out of the window.

I call Shane and tell him I can't make it. The room is quiet and the place is shrinking in on me. He and Josh come to pick me up and we go back to his place. My body feels like it doesn't quite fit right, you know? The three of us drink more marijuana tea and smoke more dope. I'm melting into the wall. I want to sleep, but it won't come. I take more Tuinals. The guys finally take me home around 9 a.m. Saturday morning. I come down so hard on the bed, I don't wake up `til Monday morning. I still have all my clothes on and my neck has a painful kink in it.

Mom's happy I'm moving home. She says I can work at the restaurant and help her out until I find an office job. Fuck, I hate it. It's long hours and Mom is running at 78 rpm and if everybody else isn't, she gets paranoid and starts acting flippos, hassling me. I have no choice, at least living at home is free.

Love,
drugged out, burned out of a job
Laura

April 24, 1970

dear mrs. wells,

my sympathies to you and your family on the death of your mother. i know she was not well towards the end. perhaps it is for the best. i know mimi couldn't help herself and it was hard on you and laura. i am thinking of you both.

"Hope is the remembrance of the future." G. Marcel

love always, kit

Laura Wells' Journal

July 15, 1989
Vista del Mar Inn
Santa Barbara
2:26 p.m.

My grandmother died on my nineteenth birthday and I didn't feel remorseful in the least. This stern matron left no imprint of loss or affection on me. It was a relief to me that she was gone; pneumonia taking her at the age of ninety-five. At the time of her death, I was strung out on Seconal—having stolen fistfuls out of a drawer in the house of a nameless record producer/drug dealer with Darcy, Shane, Josh, and faceless others. I remember thinking in my few lucid moments that now I would have a room of my own in the house I grew up in. I had always shared a room with my mother as far back as I could remember.

My whole life has been dominated by this need for space: my own carved-out niche, something I wasn't given as a child. We were always so overcrowded in Mimi's house. Uncles and aunts would appear, disappear, and reappear, finding temporary havens of retreat—following failed marriages—for themselves and my cousins. To this day I hate feeling crowded, physically or emotionally.

Katharine's deeper problems are barely touched upon in these letters. I'm still amazed at how masterfully she could camouflage her own pain. Following her release from Woodley was a band-aid treatment of tranquilizers, but she failed to take them regularly, and that rented room she lived in, she told me later, was a like a jail cell. Yet she seemed at the time to be comfortable there, I thought.

Lee Chan had graduated a couple of years before us from high school. I knew from my friendship with his sister Joy, who was in my class, that he was infatuated with Katharine upon meeting her when we were at his house visiting Joy. Katharine with her white skin, petite frame, honey-colored hair, and aquamarine eyes was the perfect contrast to his yellow skin, elongated brown eyes, football player's body, and static Asian features. Lee told me, when he first noticed her, Katharine was sitting in the living room looking out at the Chans' panoramic view of Hollywood, and she appeared dreamlike—his dream of the ultimate California Girl. He wanted her then, but she'd snubbed him.

Katharine later revealed to me that while she and Lee were seeing each other, her mental condition deteriorated badly. He would get so angry at her frigidity and unresponsiveness to him that he became physically abusive and sexually degrading to her, to the point of urinating on her. She took it all and there it is, a tiny hint, in one letter, and I didn't read between the lines.

I was living in such a state of shallowness and addiction that I wouldn't have noticed the Jolly Green Giant sitting on top of me.

Chapter Four:
Threshold

July 15, 1989
Vista del Mar Inn
Santa Barbara
9:49 p.m.

The bar offers no solace as I sit and stare at the view. Rows and rows of bottles filled with amber, honey, russet, chestnut, copper, and clear ambrosias—extolled by the guy who sits next to me—refract the luminance I feel draining out of my eyes.

"Ambrosias of brilliance through a variety of eyes, eh?" says hazel eyes, tipping his whiskey sour at me. I lift my drink and smile. He takes a puff of his Marlboro. Red, soft pack. I sip my vodka tonic. It tastes like lemonade and lime, with sugar, barely notice the vodka. Stoli, I think, but I forgot to ask. He's young. Twenty-six, maybe 24. He smells of Aramis, even through the haze of smoke. No matter.

Talked to John several hours ago, it brought no solace either. He was at work . . . still. But that was normal. His tone was clipped and all business except for the constant calls interrupting us. He said he'd have to call me back. He's upset with me. Situation normal, on all fronts.

I didn't feel like waiting for John's call. I walked on the boardwalk until the sun set. Sat in the sand watching the orange ball slip into blue, lengthening as it slid into crimson and vermillion lips, smiling grandly at first, but when opened could consume the ocean, and everything with them. I wished they'd devoured me, perhaps even absolving me in an illuminating conflagration. Would I have burned fast or slow? Would I have suffered any more than I do now as I order another drink? I wonder, as I swallow that first taste of tonic—bittersweet.

"My name is Bruce," he says as his sea-green eyes drink me.

"I'm Laura," and we shake hands.

Arms hold me tight. A mouth of jasmine and patchouli tastes me—inhales me. I exhale as we stumble a little, then collapse onto the chaise lounge on my patio—a loud crash of a sound. I want to stop before I drown.

I peek outside my locked sliding-glass patio door and he's gone. It rises inside me and I run to the bathroom to vomit last night's meal. Only liquid . . . forgot to eat. The tile floor feels cool.

Crawling like Indy does when he's stalking one of his catnip toys, I reach those lives in piles and lie down on the floor next to them. I hold my head for a moment. It's not going anywhere, but the room is. I notice a blinking light on the phone. Don't remember any ringing. John—maybe. Mom—probably. I see a small journal at the bottom of the tipped-over box. Sticking out of it is a folded, wrinkled, and partly ripped letter—no lines on the page, just stark black Kit-writing. I unfold it as it unfolds me.

may 20, 1970

dear laura,

couldn't afford to stay in that room any longer. lee helped. i stayed in the uso dorm with him. but girls are not allowed. came home after a week. he moves home soon for the summer. it's over...no more. the job is...~~is too hard.~~ it's all too difficult.

alone in my room, they're outside my door again. ~~can't find enough space, i am feeling...can't~~ can't eat. can't sleep. scary being in this room, while they're out there waiting for me...to...

they knock on the door telling me to open it...but i won't...can't seem to get the energy to get up and turn the lock. it takes four steps and two long arm swings and then i must take four deep breaths before undoing it. i'm too tired.

"katharine are you in there? what are you doing? come out. please katharine. please." mom pleads.

"oh...leave her alone, betty." dad yells.

"but she can't stay in there all day and night. she's simply got to eat."

i told them i was going out this afternoon to mail this letter. see, i'm not going to stay in my room all day. then, i am going to walk around the block ten times, five times one way and five times the opposite way. that will make everything even.

during spring break when you, joy and i stayed down in newport at her parents' beach condo, did you see the blood on me while we walked among the tide pools? the wounds. . . did anybody see them? lee said i was making them up. stop pretending, he yelled before he hit me. laura . . .the knocking again.

kit

6/12/70

Dear Mrs. Taylor,

I want to apologize for upsetting you the other day. Joy and I were so depressed after visiting Kit, we felt we had to see you right away to say how much we love her. But it all just came out. We strongly feel that she doesn't belong in that place. Seeing her there was such a shock. I still can't believe it. People there are crazy. Kit isn't crazy like they are.

I know you're doing what you feel is best for her. Again, I'm sorry we upset you. Please forgive me.
Sincerely and with much love,

Laura

7/1/70
Dear Kit,

Brenda and I share a bedroom and Darcy has her own upstairs. We're just north of Melrose—old Hollywood Spanish décor with beamed ceilings, huge stone fireplace and steps with a wrought iron bannister. Josh spends practically every night with Darcy now. Brenda and I work at that car dealership as receptionists. The owner is an old customer of Mom's.

Thank God I'm out of the house—freedom!! And my aunt's step-daughter has moved in to Mimi's old room. Remember that was supposed to be my room?? Sylvia was always begging cigarettes off of me and never cleaned up after herself. Mom feels sorry for her and since her parents split up, Mom said Sylvia could move in until my aunt gets settled somewheres. Her dad won't even speak to her. God, this girl is five years older than me but a flake. A space case, bumping into things all the time, her body's black and blue. Sylvia's totally stepped out on trangs. No wonder she got kicked out of boarding school.

I think she hooks on the side because all these strange guys in the "music industry" were calling her. It tied up the phone so much we had a big fight about it. So she finally got her own. I couldn't take it anymore—her or Mom. Amazing how blind to it all my mom and her sister are. It's probably because Sylvia works at the restaurant. Mom has another slave to boss around. Mom asks me to work on weekends sometimes when she's swamped. Shit, I know how to wait tables, but Mom loves to butt in and then brag I'm her daughter.

Darcy and I are into the daily diet pill diet. We turn into a couple of motor mouths. Don't laugh, I know, I'm not fat, but I hate it even when I put on a couple of pounds. I like weighing 104. I looked at one of those weight charts that says at 5'5" I should weigh like 120 pounds—no fucking way. Anyhow, the good thing is I can stay up all night and still make it to work the next day. Only, I did catch myself falling asleep at the file cabinet the other day.

Pierre and I've been seeing a lot of each other, except when he's on tour. He says next gig he's flying me!! AND he gets the most incredible grass. Billy, the bass player's brother, deals in weed from Vietnam that is primo. Cost $35.00 for a lid!!.

How ya doing? Please write and let me know . . . if you can. Love ya, Laura

kit's diary

july 13, 1970
camarillo hospital

what hell is this? pills all the time...everyday...what time is it? she's going to die...wants to end...the time has come now...i can't, i can't, i can'tican't.

leave... leave me alone alone
full of voices....
mommy help...me
make it stop...make it go away...make him go
i don't want to...i don't. . .nononono no
dr. schildkraut talking...talking to all of us...many people inside.
tears at my mind go away go.
make this hell end.

august 12, 1970
camarillo hospital

dr. schildkraut says keep writing in this book even though don't think i can. record thoughts...can't think, spaced out, medication keeps away nightmares, sometimes. he wants me to tell.., things but, can't...

can't remember. nothing happened. didn't happen. nothing happened. hate...mother disgusted. can't remember...stop...need to remember.

september 1, 1970
camarillo hospital

dear laura,

my room has a view. i feel like i'm a bird up high in the nest of the gigantic sycamore outside my window. i can look down on the world and see everything between the bars of this untouchable nest. i must stay in it always and never try to fly out. flying isn't allowed here. besides everyone on the ward would just laugh.

the laughing...the laughing goes on and on. can't make it stop without the meds.

he laughed that night i told him i thought i was pregnant. he laughed. i can still hear his voice saying, "...no way, you're crazy, you're not pregnant and if you are, whose is it?"

i tried to fly then over the cliff, you know the place up on mulholland, but he stopped me. funny, because i thought he would stop laughing when he pushed me into the car and then i was laughing too. he pulled my skirt up and i kept laughing. he screamed at me and then it was dad screaming at me and i was eight years old again:

"shut up, shut up, don't tell —"

"but daddy, i'm going to throw up, please, don't." daddy kept on, "suck on the sucker, little girl. that's it suck on the sucker..."

i think that the men in the white coats got things mixed up. i had to bang my head against my bedroom wall that morning to stop the voices inside telling me how bad i was...am. everybody yelling at me. make it all stop. my parents stood there staring at me. dad with a beer in his hand looking amazingly sober and mom crying.

"i hate you. i wish you were dead!" i yelled.

then those men in white crossed my arms in front of me and put a jacket on me. i can still hear mom's voice whimpering as i was led into the van. "it's not my fault. it's not my fault."

kit

september 7. 1970
camarillo hospital

dear laura

oh, i have a friend on the ward at night that appears by my bedside. she has long beautiful ebony hair. my guardian angel crawls into bed with me late at night after the attendants check on us. sometimes she stands over me and prays with her hands up in the air. other times she puts her arms around me and holds me until before the sun rises. i feel protected. but she is a secret, laura. even my psychiatrist doesn't know about her.

laura. why haven't you written me?

there are so many people here in their twenties, like me. and younger. mostly. for freaking out on drugs. when i tell them i've never taken drugs, they don't believe me.

love, kit

september 18, 1970

camarillo hospital

dear laura,

why am i here and why are you there?

i had this dream last night that i was trapped, kicking and hitting
dad. i couldn't get away from him. he held me down smothering me.
someone got confused and was supposed to give me a life jacket, but instead
it was a straight jacket. i felt myself gasping for breath. was there going
to be escape from this hell? alone, no one near to help me. suddenly i was
in the sea and water was coming up over my head, the dark cold wetness
taking me. i could hear myself yelling for help. the floor nurse woke me,
said i was disturbing the other patients.

dr. schildkraut says the voices and other people i see are different
parts of me. had to hide in the corner during one of our sessions because i
saw myself running up to me and pounding my head with my fists. i cried
for me to stop then heard dr. schildkraut saying, "we have to stop now kit."

laura, i am so tired, so very tired. baby birds nested in the sycamore
tree. i loved watching their parents bring them food. i love watching real
love. it's so safe in that nest. no one can hurt them.

why still the drug-crazed weekends? write me, laura, i want to hear
from you.

love always, kit

10/1/70

Dear Kit,

Darcy and I are communicating less and less. I'm fed up with the drugs, the parties, all these friends seem like hangers on, dragging me down. I'm moving home ASAP. Brenda split up to Sacramento, last month. She met some new guy. The rent is a little too much for just Darcy and me. So, fuck it, I'm getting out of here.

Pierre and I are over too. In bed it was great, out of bed not so great. Dealing with his possessive and jealous craziness—not so great either.

Hey, are you getting my letters? Why aren't you writing? I miss you.

Love, Laura

kit's diary

october 13, 1970
camarillo hospital

less and less of the many inside me.

dr. schildkraut was saying—shock. maybe it can help this schizophrenic.

i don't know. he says we can do this together if i'll let him.

all right, yes, all right i want to let him in and let them...out. no shock. no. i'm still afraid.

then let's get on with our work, he says. all right, i say, but please hold my hand.

stroke her dark wetness
entwines with my own whiteness
rub together, like
two cats in heat. embrace her
into my mouth. suck
those breasts, large
dark round nipples,
suck for my life.
hold on tight.
in this way
she cannot know it.
be one being.
want her.

did you know dearest laura, that i'm in love with you?

january 4, 1971
camarillo hospital

dear laura,

time stands so still here. when we're allowed supervised outings, I prefer to walk the grounds. those vast green carpets, love to lie on them and roll over and over down the gentle slopes. remember how stained our white shorts would get when we were kids . . . didn't want to ever stop rolling unchecked and uncaring of any conclusion.

kitty is dead . . . lain to rest in my many sessions with dr. schildkraut. that scared little girl inside me is under control. katharine is who I've become. who I want to be now. katharine is responsible, yet vulnerable. katharine is not afraid to go forth in life, leaving behind *what cannot be undone.*

the visit with mom was difficult. she insists, still, that none of this is her fault and she is not to blame in any way. dad didn't come. dad is simply a permanent fixture in front of a TV world. then off to a bar. every night, every meaningless moment. that is <u>not</u> going to be part of my life anymore. dr. schildkraut says i can go home next month.

away from my parents is where I want to be. north in santa barbara. dr. schildkraut has some connections for me there. a job and a place to live if I want...<u>I want</u>.

"I thank heaven somebody's crazy enough to give me a daisy"

e.e. cummings

love. katharine

○

I place Katharine's small journal with the purple paisley pattern and my own loose letters down on the coffee table and sit in disbelief. Why didn't we share these things? Why couldn't she just tell me? I feel another eruption inside my gut; I head for the toilet, mostly bile. I sit on the cold floor and stare at the toilet paper dispenser in its chrome couch. Nausea returns, only dry heaves this time. I lie back against the wall facing the toilet and feel small. Meaningless.

This is the first time I've laid eyes on these words. Regret and anger are absorbed into the canary yellow walls of this general-issue hotel room. "You let her down," say these testaments to past pain and my sorrowful discovery of it in this place I never saw before forty-eight hours ago. The yellow wallpaper and matching yellow-flowered print drapes echo back: Yes, you let her down. This scrutiny of a former time lived in scenes of gaiety and denial brings forth pain—Katharine's pain of which I was blatantly blind—and my pain, which I denied by deadening it with drugs. Katharine was attracted to me because I pushed her to be daring and impulsive. It was not in her nature to be spontaneous. She was cautious, I was not. She was thoughtful, I was not.

We told each other everything . . . didn't we?

Larry Taylor, pervert and pedophile, gave me the creeps and now it is patently clear why.

Katharine's prudishness about her sex life, while I held back little, was usually discussed in a tight-lipped manner . . . details left vague.

O

Kitty and I are sleeping late; it's Christmas break. We're at my house sharing my double bed. We talk about our respective dates, connected, but not connected. She went out with Tony's best friend, Prentiss. A blind date. They doubled with Tony and that bitch Faline. Tony and I had had a fight so he asked Faline out because he knows I hate her. I accepted a date from a girlfriend's cousin. He'd grown up in Italy and is here visiting the family for the holidays. Fabrizio liked me to call him Fabulous. He wasn't.

Kitty and I both got home around 2 a.m. Prentiss brought her home a little after me. Prentiss's mother called to find out if he was on his way home yet. She sounded frantic. Prentiss was driving his parents' maroon Mercedes 280 SL. Why did parents worry so? I wondered then (but not today).

I ask Kitty if Prentiss kissed her goodnight and she says yes. I wait for her to tell me more, but she doesn't. We smell the eggs and bacon Mom is cooking from the kitchen, but we don't want to get out of bed. We feel warm and lazy underneath my old salmon-colored satin down comforter with the torn seam that Mom never gets around to sewing. I press Kitty for specifics about the date. What was Faline wearing? How did Tony treat her? Did Prentiss only kiss Kitty once, what else? She says Prentiss was drunk and she was more worried about how he would be able to drive home. She never answers my question about a second kiss.

Christmas vacation is over and I'm in the Hollywood High quad talking to Prentiss. We're both late to homeroom. He's grounded from driving for two months because he crashed the car on the way home after he dropped Kitty off at my house. He got lost, ran into a ditch, and his parents had to come and get him at 3 a.m. not far from his home, and they were furious.

I ask him how he and Kitty got along. He tells me he thought they were getting along great. They were more than making out in the Benz before he walked her up to my door, when she abruptly pushed him off of her, zipped up her dress (my Kitty had let him unzip her dress!), and said:

"Ok, that's enough," Kit had said and that was it. She had let herself out of the car and walked up to my front porch. Prentiss said he ran to catch up with her and tried to kiss her again, and she pushed him away again, loudly telling him, "Goodnight, Prentiss. Go home!" I had heard a muffled version of it from my bedroom. He felt like he was being dismissed from class.

Kitty never tells me any of this. When we talk on the phone later that night I mention that Prentiss said he enjoyed being with her. She sounds annoyed and says, "It was okay," and changed the subject.

○

Katharine, why did you have to go it alone? Maybe that's why Bett ran away all the time—from Larry. Better to go it alone than live in a world infested with perversity. And when that didn't work, she created her own little nuclear family, only to lose everything in a catastrophe. And the loss of that "everything" sucked the breath from Larry, Betty, and Katharine, laminating the awfulness of their lives into loathing and denial. It worked for a time. But Katharine couldn't be good at everything.

There's so much more we could have shared—such as my own meeting with . . . molestation. There's that word. I hate it. Abhor thinking it, saying it, remembering it. And it disgusts me, even though it was so many years ago the memory is forced to dust off its cobwebs.

My uncle the painter, long since dead, was a cousin on my mother's side. I never was interested enough to find out the exact relation, but I was raised to call him Uncle Javier. He wasn't a very famous painter, just a very black sheep. He immigrated to California from Mexico a few years after my grandparents did in the 1920s and worked in a paint factory where he "borrowed" a lot of his materials. Mother said that branch of our family had been very wealthy at one time, but lost everything in the 1910 revolution before moving to Los Angeles. Uncle Javier had grown up a spoiled brat, never thinking he should have to work for a living.

He lived in a huge room behind the factory, until his paintings started to sell at a gallery on Olvera Street. Mom claimed that Mimi subsidized him; she loved him like a son. He used to bring her gifts—perfume, flowers, and small sketches he'd made of her. They would talk and laugh. This was long before her mind began to slip.

Then Javier purchased a small duplex in Westwood and lived there until he was run over by a school bus at age 55. I felt it was fate making him pay his due.

Uncle Javier had painted some of the members of the family, like my grandfather, Gerard—a gentle Frenchman posed with his beret and walking stick—and Aunt Elena, his sister, a dowager and probably a virgin at her death at 70. Uncle Javier didn't like doing these portraits. He preferred creating still lives of fruits and flowers standing next to small dead animals. They were so detailed they looked like three-dimensional photographs of animals about to wake up and eat you.

Mother browbeat Uncle Javier until he agreed to paint me. She had a knack for manipulating men. Mother would drop me at Uncle Javier's duplex on Saturday mornings and I'd pose for a couple of hours, after which I was expected to take a bus to the restaurant and help out during the Saturday lunch crowd.

Mostly I was bored, and at fourteen hated the whole prospect of sitting still and being kept from more important social demands like sleeping late, watching TV, or window shopping on Hollywood Boulevard with Katharine. I was ambivalent about Uncle Javier, more curious about him than anything else due to the way my family excused his bohemian lifestyle and discussed his love life in hushed tones whenever I was around.

O

The smells of oil and paint thinner make me feel light headed, so I'm very fidgety. Uncle Javier is constantly adjusting me, which makes me nervous.

"No, Laura, not that way. Put your hands folded in your lap. Please stop moving! We'll never finish this thing and your mama is driving me crazy to finish this, hay dios mío!" His accented voice is very insistent, and sounds more Italian than Mexican.

It's to be a head and shoulders portrait. This particular morning he's feeling groggy from the night before. I smell the strong smell of perfume when I come in. Shocking, it's called. Mother bought it for me once. I didn't like it—too sweet. I imagine he'd had a visitor who left right before I arrived. He has a lot of women visitors, Mom says.

He tells me to remove my blouse and he'll give me a drape as he decides a bare-shouldered portrait will be best. I change in the bathroom and take my place on the chair. Uncle Javier begins arranging the drape and moving it lower around my shoulders. Then he returns to his easel and studies me for a moment. He comes over to me and re-arranges the drape; I notice his hands are shaking.

"Laura, why don't we do a little more and see how that looks?"

"Okay," I say, not understanding what he means. He loosens the drape, dark green velvet it is, and it falls to my waist.

"That's it, that's what I want. Hold it right there," he says quickly. Then he looks at me and back at the half-finished canvas. As he continues to work he seems to be looking more at me than at the canvas.

"You are so beautiful, just like my Lorraine!" I assume Lorraine is the lingering perfume I smell.

"You are really getting your old Uncle Javier excited, my dear."

He comes over to me after what seems like hours and starts to fiddle with my breasts. He holds them in his hands, his long brown fingers softly caressing them. I'm frozen like a statue and at a complete loss as to how to act. I don't believe this is happening to me.

"Just like my Lorraine's breasts, exactly." He kneels down in front of me and puts his mouth on my left nipple and runs his tongue over it and sucks. I feel goose bumps jump off my neck and shoot down between my legs; I let out a little moan. He's holding my right breast and starts to put it to his mustache-covered lips. I see the top of his head, black hair thinning—the beginning of a bald spot at the crown. He appears ancient and ugly. I bound up and scream.

"Get away from me, you dirty old man!" I shout at the top of my lungs, grab my blouse, and stumble over him as he calls after me, "Laura, don't go, we have to finish, we have to finish, Laura *mi AMOR!*" I run so fast I pass the bus stop and run up three more blocks to the next one before I finally stop and finish buttoning the last button on my blouse.

I tell myself, it's okay, isn't it? Mother has warned me to be wary of perverts and weirdos who prey on kids, probably from the time I was six years old, and if anyone ever approached me on the street or while I was playing in front of the house, to scream like a banshee. It's okay, though, he's a family member, not some stranger. I did what you said, Mom, didn't I?

I never go back. I make up some excuse to Mom; I hate going there because he smells of B.O. or he has bad breath or I would rather go to work early with her. Mother usually believes everything I tell her— even the lies. She doesn't press me to return.

Nine years later Mother and I move out of Mimi's home. Mother for years has thought the portrait containing my face and neck was lost. It's not; I had wrapped it up and stashed it under many boxes. While packing up the house unobserved, one afternoon, I take a large serrated knife and destroy the portrait, stabbing it beyond recognition and dumping it in the commercial trash bin of the market next door to us. Each stroke is a lunge of obliteration from my memory of that awful Saturday morning and the death of that stupid naïve girl. Fate already has taken Uncle Javier away, and now I erase the last essence of my humiliation.

O

Katharine and I could have helped each other in this—our shared degradation.

All those months she was in Camarillo and didn't write to me. I thought it was part of her therapy not to contact anyone from the outside. We never discussed why she didn't write. I felt there was so much about Camarillo she didn't want to discuss. So I never pressed her.

Five years later she did share some of it. The time Lee Chan came to see her in the hospital—he was all smiles and full of encouragement that she would eventually make it out of that place intact. He acted as if nothing had ever happened between them, she said. It was all in her mind, those moments of brutal intimacy that they had shared, according to him. Or the time Eric arrived sullen and sulking. He had very little to say with the exception of How's it going? Don't worry you'll be okay and I've gotta split now, bye.

I disliked the shit from the moment I met him in school. The only reason I could see that she liked him at all was his outstanding grades in our psychology class. The teacher's pet was going to be a psychologist and Katharine admired him. He ended up being an insurance salesman; maybe there's a correlation. I do know that he did abandon her, as she said, triggering her first breakdown, and I hated the son-of-a-bitch for it.

Driving forty-five minutes north to Camarillo Hospital always felt more like arriving at a resort than a mental institution. It was built in the 1930s in Spanish colonial style, Mexican actually, with an especially distinctive bell tower building. Walking the bucolic grounds reveals expansive arcades, arched doorways, and an elaborately tiled fountain in a courtyard just below the tower. Imperfect red-tiled roofs accented by decorative turrets are juxtaposed with distinctive flower-pattern grillework that encloses almost every balcony and window.

Sprawling lawns lined with pepper and jacaranda trees afford shade and enhance the serenity of this place for all of us visitors, at first. So tranquil, so pastoral—so architecturally misleading.

Joy Chan and I drive up to the hospital entrance; the sign reads:

YOU ARE NOW ENTERING CAMARILLO MENTAL INSTITUTION. PLEASE CHECK IN AT THE GUARD GATE

We do, and the guard gives us a parking pass, directing us to Ward B. I take a wrong turn and get lost. I pass a young girl about my age with long and wavy black hair and a scrubbed pink face. She wears jeans and a plain white T-shirt, and is perhaps a visitor also. Joy rolls down the window and says in her soft melodic voice, "Excuse me, can you direct us to Ward B?" The girl answers with her finger pointed in a northerly direction.

"You take a turn up ahead and then down that line of pepper trees you take a right, then a quick left and—"

"Uh, okay," says Joy, sounding as unsure as I am.

"Would you mind hopping in and showing us?" I ask, hopeful that she will. She hesitates for a moment.

"I suppose it would be all right, uhm . . . yes, okay," and she gets in the back seat of my mom's green Impala. We find our way with her help. She tells us her name is Sharon. Joy and I thank her and she says "God Bless You" before she walks away down the road.

We enter the building marked B WARD and ask a nurse attendant where we can find Kitty . . . Katharine Taylor. She guides us up the stairs to a waiting area. There are scattered lime-green naugahyde sofas against both walls, all of them full of people, some of them patients wearing hospital-issued pants, shirts, and dresses. They're all women and they look like they're waiting for someone. We wait and watch down a long hallway, where we see a small reed-thin figure in brown cords and baby-blue flat backless bedroom slippers walking towards us. Her top is taupe and baggy. Her hair, once fresh and clean, looks the color of greasy dishwater and is stuck to her head. Her face is badly broken out—red and blotchy. Joy and I greet Kitty shyly at first. She seems happy, but nervous, to see us.

"Would you like to walk for a bit?" Kitty says, and we start to walk outside. Her hands are shaking. Joy and I decided before arriving not to ask Katharine how she is doing. We say how glad we are to see her. We don't want to put her on the spot. Joy feels some loyalty to Kitty, even though Joy's brother and Kitty have broken up. Joy saw the signs of

Kitty cracking up first hand when Kitty visited Lee at the Chan family home.

We describe to Kitty how we found our way with someone named Sharon's help. Kitty looks at us and smiles.

"Sharon is a patient here and she has delusions of being a guardian angel. She likes to go around the ward blessing people. I chased her away from my bed one night." She is laughing at our incredulous stares.

We walk to the canteen, a lunch counter that is run by the patients, and sit down. I order coffee and toast, Joy orders a Coke, and Kitty asks for tea. I'm watching the patients working behind the counter, hearing the bustling of dishes and the yelling back and forth between the waitresses and cooks. Some of them appear harried and stressed-out, trying to serve the customers as in any snack bar, but something about the faces and body movements reveal something is missing. Not in every one of them, but the waitress who takes our order, for instance, says very little. She nods in understanding as we give our orders, turns around to pin up the ticket on the short-order-cook's turnstile of tickets, and yells something to him that is incomprehensible to me. She looks unkempt, bangs held off the face by a couple of black bobby-pins. They stand out as her hair is white with black roots. It's not that she or they look unwashed, it's that they all have a battle weariness about them as if they've been through some terrible ordeal and are not quite clear how to overcome it—as if functioning normally in this proving ground of a short-order world will help them along on the path of ordering their lives into a congruous reality.

I try not to let this show on my face, but I'm in such a state I can't hear Joy's and Kitty's conversation. My toast comes and there are what look like hairs stuck to it. I can tell, out of the corner of my eyes, that Kitty is watching my reaction. She starts to laugh at my stunned look.

"Laura, do you want butter on that, or jam?" Joy comments in her funny, sarcastic way. Kitty speaks to us in such a perfectly normal tone that we wonder what she is doing here. It feels like we're sitting on a college campus talking about our teachers and our classes.

Kitty tells us she has to go back now. It has only been some forty-five minutes since we arrived. But she says she has to go. Joy and I hug her good-bye. She waves to us from her second-floor window as we drive off; the window has bars on it. That's the last time I see Kitty for a while. Bars across her face are how I remember her for some months.

On the way back to Hollywood, Joy explains how her parents were unhappy about Lee's relationship with Kitty. Recently, he's just gotten over a bad experience with Faline's little sister, Becky.

Becky is pregnant and she's still in high school. She's having an abortion and Lee comes to her house one night to try to change her mind. He feels they can make things work out. They can have a future together even though he's still in college and heavily dependent upon his parents. Becky's parents call the police to eject him from their house. The Chans are ashamed of Lee's un-Chinese conduct. They don't want him mixed up with another Caucasian girl.

Joy and I decide Kitty's mother has made a terrible mistake and we're driving straight over to her place to tell her.

During the drive, Joy relates an incident to me that happened at her parents' home when Lee brought Kitty there before they broke up.

Lee and Kitty are sitting at the grand piano in the living room. Lee is trying to teach Kitty to play Chopsticks:

"Kitty was acting pretty weird," Joy says. "She's staring into space, dazed, with a far-away look, basically non-communicative. Lee is playing a few notes and then insists on Kitty repeating them on the keyboard. He forces her hand and it just falls away limp."

"'Kitty, you are going to do this with me now!' Lee says over and over, his teeth clenched. He's treating her as if she was four years old, yet she continues to sit there like a zombie. I can't take watching this anymore so I walk over to Lee and say, 'Lee what are you doing?' looking at him as if he was the crazy."

"'I'm going to get her to play this, so help me, Joy.' He was so intent on the task that he couldn't see beyond it."

"'Don't you think you'd better take her home?' I whispered to Lee. I glanced at Kitty, her face was a blank."

Kitty doesn't share this occasion with me until after we're both married, and when she recalls it we both break down into peals of laughter. The whole thing seems so inane to us, and giggling together is a favorite pastime for us. She reminds me that Lee became an attorney after failing the bar exam four times; he was one determined guy. He did marry a Chinese girl and had a daughter—only one—to the disappointment of his parents. They were hoping for more: sons.

Chapter Five:
Passages

July 16, 1989
Vista del Mar Inn
Santa Barbara
4:45 a.m.

The dark accedes to the dawn. Daylight hovers minutes away and suddenly I'm hungry, ravenous. I call room service: not available yet. My legs ache from sitting in a child's pose for too long. A painful stretch and flex of legs and limbs encourages a propped-up-on-a-pillow position where I can just drift through the mounds of pen on paper surrounding me, upholding me, possessing me. . . .

Why didn't I end up crazy like Katharine? With my intake of drugs I'm astounded that I didn't. I've forgotten so much of this time in my life, our lives. These letters galvanize me into a whole new world—our world—arousing remembrance, lots of it.

That drug-using hippie that I was took years to get over the "bad trip"—living with flashbacks for more than a decade. They'd come out of nowhere with that same adrenalin rush when coming on to a hallucinogenic drug—surging electrical shocks pulsing through me while driving too fast on the freeway. I began taking alternate routes to avoid freeways altogether, something difficult to do in Los Angeles. And then one day these daymares just stopped. Lucky me.

So many of the people I ran around with then were dying from drug overdoses. I never thought anything of it at the time other than, like all my loaded friends, that's the breaks.

"Poor Harry ate it. Yeah, I tied him off and right after, man, it was good-bye," is the common chant of Ray Phoenix, a student in college I'm dating. He's also a dealer. It's Saturday night at his family's huge brick-and-ivy-covered mansion in Hancock Park. His mother is out for the evening; his father is out for good. Ray keeps a large bowl made of brass—14 by 8 inches on a wrought-iron stand three feet high—filled to the brim with marijuana. Smoking it paralyzes me, and he becomes angry that I'm not responsive to his lovemaking, but I can't move and he proceeds, as a necrophiliac would, to please himself. Ray is rich (old Hancock Park money, he likes to say) and obsessive about dealing. He traveled to Europe, stopping in Turkey first—taking with him crystal meth and LSD camouflaged inside vitamin capsules, 50 bottles worth—this past summer of 1969 and returned with fistfuls of hash hidden in the lining of his luggage. He also returned with a brand new Burgundy Red 911E Porsche Targa purchased with drug cash in Munich.

I swallowed mescaline about two hours ago, and I watch him tie off his arm as he prepares to inject a downer cocktail of his own concoction: Seconal, Tuinal, and a touch of Meth. He taps and when his vein pops up into view he inserts the needle.

I've never seen someone shoot up before. The tracks on his arm repulse me. The mescaline has kicked in now, causing them to look like deep ravines in the Grand Canyon. I get dressed and leave, refusing to see him again. He follows me out to my faded red VW Bug; he's naked and screams at me not to go—not to leave him. I put up the window and release the brake while Ray pounds on the windshield. I start the car in neutral while it rolls out of the driveway. I'm afraid he's going to run after me and someone is going to call the police about this naked person shouting, "Stop the fucking car and get back here you bitch!"

Weeks later I notice that the occasional white, unmarked car has stopped following me and my paranoia about my telephone being tapped ceases. Three months later, Ray is busted.

Why didn't I end up dead or comatose like Karen Ann Quinlan? One night the twenty-one-year-old Karen went out for a lovely evening, perhaps even wearing a new dress she'd been starving herself to fit into. At a party—it's crowded, it's hot, it's fun—she swallows a cocktail of Valium with an alcohol chaser, or two or three, who knows? No one was ever sure. So have I. She felt dizzy while still at the party, so have I. She needed to have a lie-down, so have I. She never woke up, I always did. She was forced to remain in a vegetative state by a hospital-imposed respirator, not actually dying until after the success of a protracted court battle her parents waged for years for the right to unplug it. Her body—emaciated and frozen in a fetal position—took ten more years to die; her brain already had.

I could have been that girl. But I had my angel. Where was Karen Ann Quinlan's angel?

Mother told me, from age two on, I had a guardian angel protecting me wherever I went. And I believed her. Maybe Karen's angel was busy watching me instead of her? Katharine's mother didn't believe in angels. Katharine wanted to, but in the end, the devil was too strong for her.

Katharine and I were consistently shy about touching one another. We were tentative in our hello and good-bye hugs. I'd put my arm around her shoulders while we walked once in a while, but she held herself in check and didn't typically return the gesture. Hugs were reserved for greetings and partings and even then we made sure our pelvises did not touch. Was this a subtle clue regarding her private feelings for me—our private feelings for each other?

Last night's dream rushes upon me:

I'm walking through hospital corridors searching for Katharine. Yet it looks as though I'm walking through the apartment complex her parents lived in. I come upon her in one of the green hallways where she is lying on her hospital bed hooked up to an IV tube. She looks ill, but is quite conscious. She sees me and tries to sit up. Her smile is weak. I sit down on the bed next to her and put my arms around her with a Why? Why? She lets me hold her for a bit and does not answer. Suddenly we are lying in the bed together, still holding one another— and our pelvises do touch. I try to encompass her more tightly.

The hotel alarm jars me. I push the nine-minute delay button and I hear the train going by again as it has regularly, morning, afternoon, and evening, every day since I came here. It's steaming past so often that I don't always hear it anymore. For some reason I set my alarm to go off this morning at 6:00 a.m. in the roused time capsule of this hotel room in Santa Barbara where I've come to say good-bye to Katharine, but can't.

She vanished too soon in the dream. It's not the first time I've dreamt of us together. Several years ago it was of us lying naked in a floating bed of soft pink and white chiffon locked in a loving and sexual embrace, but it was hazy and blurry as dreams often are and by the time I realized it was Katharine that aroused my passions in this illusion, I had awakened. As the dream returned sporadically over the years, it left me wondering about my own sexual proclivities.

When I've made love to my husband lately, why have I fantasized about being with another woman?

Now, missing Katharine as I do, I conjure up the feel of her in my arms again and tell her how much I love her and kiss her. Why didn't

I do this before it was too late? Katharine, why didn't you trust me enough to share your truth?

What's *my* truth, now, by the way?

The phone rings, it's John. He wants to know what the truth is too. As in how long I'm going to stay holed up in this crypt by the sea. I wish I knew.

"Laura, how long is this going to go on?"

"I can't say exactly, a few more days."

"Why?"

"You don't understand, do you?"

"No, explain it to me."

"Look, John, I have an opportunity here to understand my life, Katharine's life—our lives starting back over twenty-six years ago. I have a cache of letters and diaries that need to be read. It means something. We both saved them for a reason. I can't come back until I've finished all of it."

"I think this whole thing is mentally unsound. You're making Katharine's death an obsession. She was a very unstable person. You helped her all you could, but you have your own life to live."

"God, John, it's only been four days. Give me some time, will you?!"

"Fine, what does that give me?"

"Space and distance, something we both need from each other."

"Great, that's just great. Okay, that editor called again, whatever her name is from Outside/In . . . . whatever. You'd better call her back. She sounded a bit piqued on the answering machine."

"Yes, all right, look, I'll call you later, okay?"

"Yeah, sure, one of these days."

"John, please—"

He hangs up.

My truth lies somewhere between epistolary stacks one, two, and three scattered around me. An accumulation of what was, and what is. All I'm missing is what will be. Which stack—as in the game of blackjack, and which card—do I pull from? Which will make me feel whole again? I'm the dealer here, I decide or, has it already been decided for me . . . I pull the yellow—that color that supposedly stimulates intellectual thought—yes, the legal-length sheet of yellow paper with red lines on it. I hunker down and begin again to read, following the yellow path bordered in red and inscribed in black and blue where it takes me.

6/21/72

Dear Katharine,

Working at a TV station is such a trip. I saw Bob Hope and Lucille Ball yesterday. Everyone acts real casual about celebrity sightings as it happens a lot.

The people in accounting are anything but conservative. So many women here still believe in banning the bra. Truth is, I don't need one. When we're bored some of us girls play the pencil test. I always pass. A pencil never sticks to my rib cage, when placed just underneath my breasts. Those number two leads fall to the floor hard.

Anyway, the film editors down the hall and I got high on our lunch hour yesterday in the park across the street from work. Paul (gay) and Ernie (married), real sweethearts. They tell me how great my boobs look (I'm glad I joined that gym). We're all going in on a spoon of cocaine. It's not my thing, but I thought I'd try it—costs about $100 split 4 ways.

I'm happy you're settled in Santa Barbara at the boarding house. I hope your job at the—was it an architectural firm?—makes you happy.

Moving home has saved me lots of money, but Miss Space Case Sylvia still lives here. She pays absolutely no rent, goes from job to job getting fired or quits. Mom just makes excuses for her. Plus she's in the room that should've been mine, God damn it! So here I am 21 years old and still bunking with Mom! Darcy and Bruce are getting married in July. I guess their VD finally cleared up, last time I heard they'd bounced it back and forth 6 times. I'm not invited to the wedding. Funny, huh? Hell, I introduced them! Ce la vie.

Love you, Laura

P.S. Don't worry, I sold my portion of the coke to another girl—not my thing.

December 5, 1972
Santa Barbara

Dear Laura,

I've met someone. His name is David Fields . . .a friend of a friend. He knows about my being in Camarillo and it's okay with him. He told me about being in jail as a teenager. He was busted for smoking one joint and it's okay.

He is blonde, trim, and medium height with big saucer blue-green eyes. David is three years older than I am and comes from an alcoholic family too. I like him.

Mom came up and spent the day last Saturday without Dad again. We started out having a good time. She took me to lunch and saw where I was living. Then she says,

"Are you sure you're feeling all right? I mean you're not upset about anything, are you?" She went on like this until she left on the 4 o'clock Greyhound.

I'm glad we don't see each other often. She did leave me $100 though.

I haven't introduced her to David yet, but I told her about him and she hopes he is a "nice boy." She thought Eric was a nice boy. Laura, be careful with the drugs, please.

"The press of my foot to the earth springs a hundred affections."
Whitman
Love always, Katharine

4/1/73

Dear Katharine,

I'm interviewing for the production assistant job on The Weekly Show. It's a news magazine format. They travel around the city with the talent doing interviews about different people and places. Production is where I want to go. I've become friends with one of the other production assistants and she notified me about an opening. Also, she introduced me to this beautiful guy named Terry, he was in Vietnam. Another blonde, freckled, 6'4" with a square cut jaw and a terrific bod. We went out on a blind date and after dinner I went home with him. He is so cuuute! It's funny-strange, because he refused to go all the way. He'd only kiss and hold me. I was kidding him about how all he wanted was a quick fuck, earlier at dinner. He had to prove himself, I suppose. By the second date he changed his mind.

Katharine, I want this job. I'll have to work my butt off as it's long hours and taping every Sunday, sometimes even Saturdays. But it's show biz, and besides there are a lot of good-looking men to meet. So wish me luck, please.

Love you, Laura

August 12, 1973
Surface Edge Inc.
Santa Barbara

Dear Laura,

Sometimes I question whether moving in with David was the right thing to do. I love him, but we have to share with his brother Steve, his brother's girlfriend Shana, and Steve's girlfriend's best friend Emily.

It's a three-bedroom house we're renting and a fairly good size, but I feel so cramped at times.

Shana is pregnant, it's not Steve's though. Emily is getting over a bad marriage. Steve and David are extremely close.

David likes living in a house because of the dogs and cats. We just couldn't make it on his mechanic's salary and my salary alone.

He is working on an idea for opening up a halfway house. He is talking to the city about the plans and trying to raise money. He wants to help people like he was helped. It scares me, a little. People coming out of jail, who qualify, will be able to stay in the house to give them time to re-adjust to the outside world. David feels strongly it will work and won't give up until he's succeeded. Everyone living with us will be involved; I guess that means me too.

I am keeping my job though. I need that security, it's not much, but I enjoy working in the office with creativity all around me. I've got to run and catch my bus.

Love always, Katharine

11/22/73

Dear Katharine,

I enjoyed meeting David, he appears to be very much in love with you. I'm sorry Thanksgiving was such a drag at your parents'. Holidays have been spoiled for me ever since I've had to work at Mom's restaurant. Running ragged, waiting on tables of obnoxious customers demanding more dressing or wine or sending back their plates with,

"Oh miss, I'd like another cup of coffee please?"

or

"Hey little girl, will you please bring me a doggie bag?"

or

"Excuse me miss, the bathroom is out of toilet paper."

or

"This bill is incorrect!"

Mom still insists that I help her of course; the guilt trip she lays on me if I refuse is the usual sad face, disappointment in the eyes and "...I've helped you when you needed it, you can darn well do the same for me!" I hate it but I have to, because she's right and I still do live with her.

I can't tell you how many times Terry and I have stopped by on a date, and Mom has begged us to take a delivery to a customer (we don't do that anymore). Then she's bugging us to let her come along when we're on our way out to dinner. Terry doesn't say anything because Mom pays, but I know it's getting old for him because it is for me too. See how lucky you are that you don't have to deal with your parents that often.

Terry's moved back home to save money and our time alone is special—thank God he drives a van. It's come in handy when there's nowhere else to go.

One night we were so loaded and horny that we parked in front of that monastery in the Hollywood Hills and spent the night there. Sacrilegious, but we felt safe.

I didn't get the job, damn it. Somebody's friend got it instead. They told me next time an opening comes up to try again. Wasn't meant to be this time. Mom always says: that which is yours, no one can take away from you.

Love you, Laura

○

When I first meet David I don't care for him, at all. Katharine brings him to the house one evening. I'm alone. Mother is working; that no-account Sylvia is out with another nameless face.

The three of us sit and chat on the sofa in the living room for an hour or so. David looks unkempt and average. As he speaks, I notice his simplicity of language, dirt under his fingernails, worn hiking boots, and long straggly hair. Yet his eyes glow when they fall upon Katharine. Yes, he loves her, he has fallen for her the way Lee had.

Katharine attracts men who want to touch her, take care of her, save her; however, some of them can't read the sign in the box above her head, "Fragile. Handle with care!" Like cartoon characters created by a cartoonist, wouldn't life be simpler if we human beings could read the boxes above each other's heads, the true subtexts of our lives. If we were able to know what another is truly thinking, how much time and energy people could save in dealing with each other!

David strikes me as driven, self-motivated, self-centered. All he talks about is his halfway house and how hard he works. I feel he doesn't credit Katharine entirely for her contribution to the relationship, or his project. I am prone to snap judgments, but I feel I'm right on this one. She looks happy but ambivalent about their future; the halfway house takes so much time and effort for them, she says. She feels it's a burden, at times. He clearly feels elated by the work he is doing there.

"Somebody's gotta give these people a chance, you know," David offers. "Society would jus' like to forget about 'em. You give a guy from prison half a chance he won't disappointcha, not the ones that really wanna change, ya know?"

I can see that Katharine is not committed in the same way. She goes along with it to please David. I am impressed with his dedication to humanity, something I'm too selfish to ever attempt. I don't care about that part of life and think David is crazy to deal with life's underbelly in that way. I think how Katharine doesn't need that kind of stress in her difficult life. I find myself listening with half-an-ear while she recounts the problems they encounter in helping rehabilitate lost souls. I'm not a winner in the compassion department.

It seems that David's desires and wants come first, and Katharine comes second. I try to like him as the years pass, but I'm not successful. Terry tries too. They only meet a few times and never really get to know one another.

○

Remembering the blinking light, I dial Mom's number. My stomach seizes and a fist of nausea hits, then calms, as I swallow some tea with milk. Mom answers and assures me:

"I didn't mean to bother you."

"Yes, Mom, I know."

"*Mija*, why don't you ever come and see me . . . you never do . . . no you don't. I know you don't like me. You really don't, you don't even know me, you know nothing at all about me—"

"Mom, did you forget that Ana told you Katharine died?"

"*Quién*, who's that?"

"Mom, my best friend from eighth grade, come on, you remember her: Kitty!"

"*Hay sí sí sí*, Kitty, is that the girl from . . . from . . . from, *como se llama?*

"Camarillo."

"Oh yes . . . how is she, *mija?*"

"She's dead, Mom."

"Whaaaaat? Is that possible? Why not me? *Por favor*, why not . . . I keep faxing God, and he doesn't answer. Laura when are you coming, please, I need you, please come to see me, please."

Ana gets on the phone to tell me Mom has been crying on and off all day. Ana has given her another pill for the interminable itchiness Mom suffers. Fractured nerves, from no longer being in control of her life, create a relentless need for Mom to tear away at her skin, leaving large gouges that redden and scab over. The worst is on her face, arms, legs, and shoulders—the areas easily reached. No matter how much ointment the doctor prescribes, how much Ana trims her nails, or how much we all tell Mom to stop scratching, she refuses. Picking at her skin is an involuntary reflex. She's unaware of the damage she's doing, she says. She forgets that it's bad for her, she says. She wonders why she has such "bad little things" crawling on her skin to torture her. Ana says she has caught Mom plucking away at her arms and face with tweezers that Mom keeps hidden just for this masochistic cleansing ritual. Ana takes the tweezers away then finds Mom scoring her chest and neck with a kitchen knife; Ana takes that away and finds Mom scraping her legs with a potato peeler; Ana removes that instrument of torture and finds Mom clawing at her arms with a plastic fork. Mom has these implements of laceration hidden all over the house.

It's necessary to dig out and destroy the prickling sensations that plague her. As a result, Mom has insomnia exacerbated by the near-scalding hot showers she insists on taking when Ana's not looking even though the doctor has told her repeatedly to take cool ones. Sometimes Ana is awakened by Mom stumbling into a chair or knocking a TV tray onto the carpet on her way back to bed—her skin dappled and still bleeding. Ana puts the healing salve on Mom's body and scolds her for the ruin Mom is making of her skin. To Mom this is not just a purification practice, it's scrubbing off the skins—and the sins—of her past. Scratch marks mar her body—expiation through scarification of what she has left: a small, skinny, almost skeletal body, with a brain that wants relief . . . release. So I ask:

"Mom, why do you hurt yourself like that?"

"One day you'll be my age and . . . and you'll think of me, I promise you, and *you'll* see, just wait." I can almost see her head shaking up and down 100 miles away here in Santa Barbara.

I ask her the same question again about this rite of self-mutilation. She swears for the fourth time in her Sybil-says-beware voice that "*you will see, when you think of me when you are old.*" She can't help herself. One of our family legacies is that if a spoken phrase sounds good once, then repeating it again and again is even better. So there'll be other days that this conversation will go beyond this point, but not today. This is as far as I will let it go.

My eyes burn, my mind blurs, but I can't stop reading. Room service keeps me going. The young man carts in the table full of refreshment amongst my room piled with papers, an unmade bed, and more clothes on the floor than on me. I haven't changed out of my robe all day. My breakfast dishes still littered with bits of potato and uneaten fruit, are retrieved with a look of puzzlement. He asks no questions. I eat so little. This morning I barely managed an English muffin with strawberry jam. Weak tea is all I can stomach.

I still cannot grasp that they are mine or Katharine's: these letters like paintings covered and left in an attic undiscovered for many years, strangers that I dimly recall seeing before when hung and admired— but still alien and long out of fashion. Or characters in a nascent story of mine not yet thoroughly explored, possibly. There's a seed here for a body of short stories. There is. I must finish consuming every last boxful of correspondence . . . content.

What will I see next?

I come upon a photograph of Katharine and myself around the ages of seventeen and (me) almost sixteen. I'd spent the night at her apartment. We're standing next to the ironing board. The iron peeks out from behind Katharine's shoulder. She wears that wide-lapelled white-and-olive-green flower print jacket with a white knit turtleneck underneath purchased at Broadway Hollywood. I'm wearing a royal blue knit minidress with cap sleeves and gold buttons (feeling quite the grownup), purchased at Knobby Knits on Hollywood Boulevard, a shop then considered tasteful and expensive. We'd shopped for each outfit together that weekend, buying them with Katharine's allowance money and my restaurant wages.

My hand rests upon her shoulder. We're standing close. She's wearing some drop-bead pierced earrings. I have a black-banded Timex watch on my right wrist. We're a stark contrast. Her short blonde pixie haircut with long bangs slightly covering her eyebrows, allowing her long eyelashes to swallow those balmy half-open guileless blue eyes. My black chin-length hair is pushed back away from my face with a black ribbon headband, exposing my grandmother's forehead of two hardly discernible bumps just below my hairline, wisps of hair framing my forehead. My angular face with two black spinels for eyes that appear to know more than they do, topped with unruly black eyebrows, virgins to any tweezers.

Until the next weekend spent at my house when Katharine almost plucks all of my eyebrows off.

When does the pain go away?

Chapter Six:
Approach

Laura Wells' Journal

July 16, 1989
Vista del Mar Inn
Santa Barbara
1:13 p.m.

I hold it in my hand. I stand next to him and my eyes are closed. I don't enjoy seeing this 8x10 in living color. Maybe that's why I stashed it in this box this morning, only to have his gaze hold me once again like it did then.

The Golden Gate Bridge lies in the background, insignificant as an Erector Set piece left askew on top of a pile of clothes. The big span looks like it's growing out of the right side of my head. Even in the early '70s smog has already appeared in the air over the city. Terry has entered the picture, all six-feet-four of him. Uncle Barnie calls him long, tall, strong, and silent. He is 22 and an artist who loves to paint and take photographs. He also makes furniture out of wood and Plexiglas that decorates our apartment back home. He holds me in his right arm and I rest my arms on top. Uncle Barnie says "Hold it, that's right, well okay, hold each other then." The Hasselblad shutter clicks. I blink as I relish the eroticism of this moment with this boy who returned home safe from Vietnam, with this boy who prefers not to discuss what he experienced there unless he's stoned or drunk, with this boy who loves me so and I him . . . or at least I tell myself this. At least he is intact from his war experience, or at least I tell myself this also. I blink away the fact that almost two years have elapsed since his return from duty on an oil tanker in the South China Sea and, before that, shore duty near Danang.

Terry and his years prior to meeting me just don't exist in my mind. But when we smoke enough grass, drink enough wine, drop enough mescaline, fragments of war spew forth . . . a night on patrol with an ARVN unit scouting VC. Shots fired, clips emptied into a family inside a hut, babies included, consumed by fire—all. These shared memories, this on-and-off stream of 'Nam replays and flashbacks, will disrupt the cloud of my innocence as his guilt burns through inhaled Marlboros-in-a-box and more hits of grass. Mornings after we will recall little of such nights and what was revealed. He will forget just for the sake of forgetting, at least that is what I tell myself. I will also tell myself that it is all part of the purple haze, part of the '60s surreality that was also the '70s. I will return to my comfort zone, maintaining a naive posture about the world, about Vietnam, about the War, about Terry's participation in it, about my (non)participation.

Some fifteen years later, I haven't been thinking of myself back then as part of the Vietnam Generation. No, I'm all Sixties Generation: Freedom Summer, Free Speech Movement, massive war protests, altered states and alternative life styles—a counterculture. Yet I will wonder, were those images representative of the time? Or were they just the creation of the media focusing on the bizarre, the crazy—and the threatening. Or were they what I want to remember, want to perceive about a time so long ago?

My tears will flow when I read the works of Michael Herr's *Dispatches*, a very personal journal written by a war correspondent for *Esquire*, one of the first works to convey how different and surreal this warfare was from any other; Philip Caputo's *Rumor of War*, the experience of a young Marine Lieutenant and college graduate who answered President Kennedy's challenge to "Ask not what your country can do for you. . ." with enthusiasm, only to end up in a muddy foxhole in Vietnam, raging in despair in the muck and the quagmire; and Tim O'Brien's short story "The Things They Carried," a shocking and visceral rendering of the heaviness of surviving in a booby-trapped jungle, in a booby-trapped war. My tears will flow in the middle of an afternoon read of O'Brien's work alongside Katharine.

I will stammer " . . . I . . . I only wish I had known . . ." and admit the sense of betrayal I will feel to this man, a member of the Vietnam Generation, who just wanted to give something back to his country. I will painfully admit that I ignored and dismissed that service as much of the rest of the country did back then—welcoming back our veterans with disdain and derision, calling them "baby killers," the traitorous enablers of a criminal war. They received no banners, no parades, and no keys to the city.

Terry and I don't share such thoughts on that occasion, though. But we do share cigarettes, joints, Mateuse, a passion for camping, and making love. I only know him as the cute guy on the blind date I met through a mutual friend at KNXT where I have worked for about a year. This friend warned me that Terry had been getting into one too many bar fights since his discharge from the Navy. But I am blind to Terry's anger—at least until it escalates and our partnership stops surviving our differences. He wants more than I am capable of giving. He wants the steadiness of marriage and the hope of more. I want no such thing.

At 22 years of age, I'm working in television in hope of more. I am not ready for Terry's definition of commitment. Such dissonance will bring many bumps in the road of our relationship. I will not become his possession. Scenes of jealousy and fearsome arguing will bring dishes smashing onto the kitchen floor. And so, following our breakup a year later, I will not be stunned when my red VW Bug disappears from the driveway of my mother's home on a Sunday afternoon and turns up a few days later, abandoned on a nearby street with the front end caved in, nor will I be surprised to find his signature pack of Marlboro Reds in my glove compartment.

Since our initial meeting, and despite the Paris peace accords, protests against the war still occur, but neither of us participates. When Terry left Vietnam, as he often reminds me, troop strength was approximately 152,000; U.S. dead 45,543. He was still there during Kent State where four students were killed and nine wounded by the Ohio National Guard; but he was back home during the subsequent May Day protest in Washington aimed at paralyzing the government by clogging Washington roads and shutting down offices, which got ten thousand protesters arrested. Their slogan was "If They Won't Stop the War, We'll Stop the Government." More than five thousand D.C. police officers, fifteen hundred National Guardsmen, and eight thousand federal troops made mass arrests as an estimated fifty thousand protesters swarm through the streets, starting fires and blocking traffic, and making commuters and bureaucrats arrive hours late for work. The police arrested people without noting names or details of alleged offenses—like herding two thousand protesters into RFK Stadium. Then a judge ordered authorities to justify the dragnet arrests or release the suspects. The courts threw out almost all the arrests, Terry tells me.

Terry watched every bit of that news coverage, I did too, but I was stoned through most of it. He tells me how he rooted for the protestors. "Damn right," he said, downing a swig of Coors. We talk of watching the television coverage when Veterans Against Vietnam threw their Purple Hearts, Silver Stars, and Bronze Stars over a barricade around the Pentagon. Terry hooted, "Go! Yeah! Don't blame any one of them, if I had 'em I'd do it too."

We smoke and talk for hours. Terry in particular shares the despair and rage of these vets, who look more like hippies than soldiers, throwing their badges of bravery and honor at the symbol of their betrayal. Terry wipes a tear at this. I take a drag off my Sherman.

We watch repeats of films like *The French Connection* and *Dirty Harry*, Terry's hero. Terry does not read much, but he draws and paints a lot. Attending art classes at night, Terry likes to create serene and quiet landscapes.

We watch *All in the Family* once in a while, otherwise *Monday Night Football* viewing is a religion for Terry. Sunday mornings are spent playing football at his former high school where he and his friends climb over the chain link fence, throwing passes and making touchdowns. The shirtless team plays the shirts. Terry prefers the shirtless team, where each of his finely hewn muscles ripples as he throws a pass.

But for now, in this eternal moment in this old picture, we sit on a rail on a street with the Golden Gate Bridge behind us in picture-postcard view. He wears a short jean jacket that matches the cerulean of his eyes. A small breeze passes us and playfully rearranges his hair; I can almost see it moving on the surface of the picture. A month from now, when I show the photo to a co-worker, she will say that I am being upstaged by Terry's good looks. Most of my girlfriends and co-workers will say they think this boyfriend is strikingly handsome, punctuated by his kind heartedness and caring manner. They compare him to Robert Redford in *Downhill Racer*. This, in part, is why I fell for him also. He swept me off my feet on our first date. He was cordial, gentle, affectionate, entranced with me, and I with him. We ate dinner, smoked, and talked for hours. When we said goodnight, I learned what it felt like to be kissed in midair as he literally lifted all five-feet-five of me, in my floor-length leather coat, up to meet his lips.

In the photograph my black hair is pulled back and hangs long past my shoulders. The tips are brown from the sun with a little peroxide help. I wear a borrowed plum-colored shirt with brown pinstripes. It's ugly. It's left over from my bad breakup with Pierre, my rock band man whose clothes I used to share because he was skinny too. As usual, I wear no bra. I had burned it as did all my other girlfriends (actually we just left them unused in a drawer).

We are driving home from a Canadian vacation. It's summer and we've been almost three weeks on the road. We took Pacific Coast Highway north as far as we could and eventually stayed with a friend in Vancouver. Now we are on the return leg and have stopped in San Francisco to visit Uncle Barnie and his new girlfriend before returning to Los Angeles and our respective jobs. Uncle Barnie never leaves any event photographically undocumented. But at his portrait studio in

San Francisco, he only photographs business executives: CEOs, CFOs, and the like.

Uncle Barnie likes my boyfriend because he is so polite, soft-spoken, and respectful. Although Uncle Barnie says I am obviously the one in charge of the relationship, he likes this guy all the same. Uncle Barnie is also a veteran: he was in the Navy during World War Two. In the fall Terry will take classes on photography, and he'll work with Uncle Barnie a little in his portrait studio on yet another one of our vacations. Uncle Barnie, thinking we might marry, offers to eventually turn over the studio to Terry, so we can have a future.

Three years from now this ex-boyfriend and I will run into each other at the wedding of a mutual friend. I will also see my ex-boyfriend from the rock band there. These two exes are casually acquainted with each other. The three of us will chat, smoke, drink, and laugh together while celebrating the wedding of our friends, and then go our separate ways. I will not see Terry again. Pierre will attend my wedding the following year. I will attend his wedding three years after that.

O

Lying on the chaise lounge on my patio at the Vista del Mar Inn, I rest my head back and relish the persistent sound of breaking waves in the breezy soft heat of this Sunday. I stare past the white fly-specked shades swaying just inside the sliding glass doors and draw in the salt and the sea. I glance at a sign the hotel has posted along the tracks to look like a train stop.

To San Francisco 375 m.
Vista del Mar elevation 21 feet

Hotel beachgoers pause to rinse in the outdoor shower. They rub themselves vigorously after with white clean towels while standing on the gray plank deck of the oceanfront thoroughfare. I look beyond the gray railing and appointed wood lamp posts, beyond the royal blue patio dividers between rooms, and beyond the stand-out matching blue-tiled roof always noticeable from the highway. I study the rows of ramshackle cottages and apartments that travel up the coast, perhaps all 375 miles to San Francisco. My eyes are drawn back to another hotel sign that reads:

Beach Rentals Available:

Beach Umbrellas
Beach Chairs
Boogie Boards
Chaise Lounges

See Attendant

Everything a mother would need for a day at the beach with her child, plus an attendant to boot. By the looks of the elderly gentleman behind the outdoor bar (non-alcoholic drinks only), he appears to need an attendant of his own.

Another sign states:

Parents do not leave children unattended
Vista del Mar Inn will not be responsible

And, last, a sign that announces:

No Lifeguard On Duty

Just what I need, a lifeguard, but he's not on duty. A lifeguard right now, in this place, in this moment, would be helpful to tell me what to do next—someone else to take responsibility for my unattended thoughts that need attending. How do I continue? Should I continue? Should I not? What should I do?

Terry was my lifeguard back then, only he expected me to dive into the depth of his emotions and swim to his core, without acknowledging what a treacherous swim it would be. Unlike a mother watching over her child playing at the beach and cautioning her not to go in the water right after she's eaten, I would just tell her to leap in, although as her mother I would be right there with her treading the same wave. Terry *was* the wave. And I was no mother. I was the child. And this child wasn't ready for such engulfment.

I close my eyes and hear a seagull call. I recall hearing a similar call while walking on a similar beach when Terry and I spent an afternoon with David and Katharine. I recall so many afternoons.

○

Terry thinks David is just a very simple guy like himself. We'd
eaten at a café on the beach nearby, not far from this beach at the del
Mar, when Terry and I drove through Santa Barbara on our way to
Canada for that vacation. David and Katharine are standing near the
water, testing the temperature with their toes. Terry and I are walking
past them along the waterline, agreeing that David's table manners
are just slightly lacking. We had watched David shovel his lunch into
his mouth like there was a timer on it that was going to beep any
moment and make his plate disappear whether he was done or not.
Then we watched (trying not to look disgusted) as he sucked whatever
food was left off each of his fingers with loud smacking noises, then
cleaned his fingernails with a fork. I thought I was going to lose my
lunch. Katharine and I break into a jog to get ahead of the guys. I ask
Katharine how she can handle David's boorish behavior.

"David says that if people can't accept him for what he is then
that's too bad!" she answers. She's tried, she says, to encourage him to
clean up his eating habits, but to no avail. It amazes me that she can
overlook that sort of thing. I make sure that we . . . that I never have to
eat with him again.

On the occasional weekend Katharine visits me, usually by herself.
She makes the obligatory visit to her parents, but doesn't want to stay
with them. With me, she briefly gets away from them and the pressures
of her life with David. I love it when we sit on either end of my sofa,
our sock-covered feet stretched out in front of us. Sometimes we even
pull our nightgowns down over our knees, making us look as if we
owned huge bulbous breasts, and talk and laugh late into the night,
sharing like we did as kids.

○

Katharine and I are in my bathroom brushing our teeth. It's one of
those weekends we both cherish, quality time for both of us we wish
could last forever. This time it's a school holiday on Monday, so we
don't have to part on Sunday. We're looking at ourselves in the big
mirror over the bathroom sink. She's giggling while she looks at herself.
I see why, she has brushed the toothpaste past her bottom lip onto
her chin. The Crest is dripping down it. The same Crest is foaming
on my lips and on my braces. We're both laughing at ourselves with

our toothpaste goatees and mustaches: euphoria from the most trivial source, and a momentary sense of relief from the futility of our lives.

O

We're sitting on the living room sofa at the new house Mom and I have just purchased. Mom convinced me this would be a wise investment, especially after my difficult breakup with Terry. Katharine and I are having a cup of tea as she describes her dysfunctionally functional in-laws.

"Laura, why did things have to be the way they were? Why do they still?" she asks.

"Because they couldn't be any other way, I guess. Things are just meant to be, we have a choice, but we also have our destiny."

"I don't know, sometimes, I really don't. Shana is starting to drink now. She's racked with guilt, I think, over the birth of her baby. She used Seconal through part of her pregnancy and is uptight about the effects on her son. Steve ends up being the baby's mommy and it's not even his child. The father's in prison somewhere and doesn't even know the baby exists. Shana is so stupid. David tells her to cool it and she won't listen and she walks all over Steve."

I can't understand why Katharine puts herself in the position of being surrounded by more dysfunctional people with alcoholic backgrounds. But she desperately needs a family involvement and (she once calls it) "communicative dynamics." Her parents don't know what communication is. At least with David and the rest, Katharine finds an odd family unity.

At least Mom and I divested ourselves of the family hangers-on: Sylvia moved out with a music producer, and her mother remarried. Mom and I finally lived together alone—but not for long.

Katharine voices her trepidation as to the direction of her future with David and her anxiety about making ends meet. David is confident that the means will be available to achieve whatever ends he chooses. Katharine is not that secure. And in that first year at school, neither was I. Katharine is a big part of the insecurity, and a lot of uncertainty. Who is she? Who was she?

O

We're standing in the school quad of Le Conte Junior High. Katharine is behind me waiting to see what my first attempts will bring, and then she will follow if the coast is clear. A boy we're both in love with, Jesse Jameson, is standing by the snack window. He has green eyes that shoot electricity at you, a peaches-and-cream complexion and dark brown straight hair with bangs that collide with his equally dark and thick eyebrows. He's wearing his blue Pendleton. To look at him makes our hearts pound. Katharine is keeping her distance until I call her over and introduce her.

"Jesse, you know Kitty, don't you?" That will be her cue to approach and we can ask him if he's going to the Christmas dance.

At the dance it's ladies' choice, and it's a slow dance, Johnny Mathis singing *Chances Are*. I'm the first girl to cross over to the line of boys and pick a partner. I want it to be Jesse, but Jane has beat me to it, so I pick Greg—a kid who stars in TV commercials, and has red hair and a crush on me. He holds me close. He smells of Russian Leather. I watch Kitty lean against the wall of the gym looking tiny and distant in her jade green satin dress with the big white sash and bow in the back. We are both wearing black patent leather squash heels. It makes me taller than Greg. Kitty stays in place watching Jesse dance with Jane. I smile at Kitty; she waves her fingers at me without moving her hand. She won't ask a boy to dance, never allowing herself the possibility of a refusal. Until I knew her better, I thought she was extremely stuck-up. The truth is she is very shy and I misread this in the beginning, as do most of our other friends.

○

She sends out these mixed signals her whole life—I'll never know what her whole life would have been. Her whole life . . . sounds like a phrase for someone who at least makes it into their sixties or seventies. Katharine barely made it to forty—that girl who sent me needlepoint in black frames and white frames along with quotes from Bob Dylan's *Blowing in the Wind*; who sent me napkins sewn on her sewing machine, every stitch full of time and effort and by her love. That girl is gone and I will not receive any of these things again. All her homemade earthiness was housed within a spirit as delicate as a spider's web washed away in an early morning rain.

I should have learned Katharine's fine art of disguising one feeling for another as a teenager. I was what I was, all out there. "Let it all hang out," was my motto. Honesty was the best policy, I thought. But it came out of me more like bluntness, or just having a plain big mouth. I didn't know any better.

I was my mother's daughter in this regard. Mom spoke her mind whenever and wherever she felt like it. What I didn't notice as a child was the questioning looks people gave her—and me—when she did this and I continued to be outspoken from childhood into young adulthood. Discretion was not something I learned from my mother. I didn't know I needed to learn it. Katharine never insisted that I should. She accepted me as I was; never criticizing, never moralizing. I wanted to shake her loose from the rigidity of her parents, her life, and her standards. She was brought up to respect rules. I assumed rules were there to be, if not broken, skirted around. My mother made her own rules. She was independent and answered to no one. Katharine's mother answered to an inept alcoholic husband.

○

It's 1967; we're attending a slumber party at Penelope Levin's house. It's in the Hollywood Hills and is full of antiques. Her mother makes puppets, which line the shelves instead of books. Penelope plays the harp and has her own suite of rooms, so we can be loud and noisy and her parents won't be able to hear us. We attend different high schools, but know each other through Pierre's band. Penelope is a friend of Pierre's sister. We all decide to raid the liquor cabinet. I'm one of the leaders in this operation, encouraging everyone to follow. Katharine stands by and observes. I get smashed to the point of throwing up all night in Penelope's bathroom with the groovy old-fashioned black and white octagonal floor tiles. Some of the other girls do too. Katharine is there, sober, mopping foreheads with a wet towel—my forehead and those of several other girls. Maybe, just maybe, she has taken a drink from half a glass of vodka, maybe a small sip even, but she never loses control of herself or gives in to extreme behavior . . . at least not yet.

April 25, 1974
Santa Barbara

Dear Laura,

You must be happier in that new house. I've been feeling pretty down. . . well . . . David's had an affair with Shelby, one of the girls that work in the halfway house. One of the guys who work there told me after he'd had several beers one night when we were working late. I confronted David. He said it happened a couple of months ago and it was a one-time fling and besides he was drunk. This hurts . . . I mean, what am I supposed to feel, you know? Why should being drunk excuse anything?

This halfway house is taking every amount of energy and blood that we can spare and that's not much. I keep tabs on the books; David has to beg for more funding. When I tell him we are short on funds, he acts as if he doesn't believe me.

We've been getting heroin addicts who break our rules, get hooked back on the drug, and one of them stole a typewriter out of the office. David doesn't like to take them in, but sometimes there's nowhere else for them to go. Mom and Dad came up for a visit last weekend, for the day. Dad has cut back, only beer. His doctor told him he had to.

The visit was tense. David can't stand my dad. They came to the house. Mom kept commenting on how nice it was even though "there are so many people living here," she said, "it must be difficult, how do you manage?" After lunch they drove back to L.A.

I'm so glad I live up here and they live down there.

"Life is a complicated business fraught with mystery and some sunshine."

P. Roth

Love always, Katharine

P.S. Sorry about you and Terry, but it's what you wanted, wasn't it?

9/18/74

Dear Katharine,

I re-interviewed for the Production Assistant job and...I got it! They decided to hire another one since the show is doing so well. I'll be making, with overtime, around $15,000 a year. I am so excited. I start in October. Hooray!! No more boring accounting. I'll be running around assisting the producer and assistant producer. It's really a gofer job, but has potential for bigger and better!!

Interesting development: I've been dating one of the salesmen down the hall; he comes into accounting to check on his accounts occasionally. He's Colombian and black! Anyway, we were talking the other day about dancing—how much we both enjoy it—and he said we ought to go out dancing sometime. So the following weekend, we went to this place downtown. It's kind of a sleaze, but one of the girls at work mentioned going there and that the music—a cross between Latin jazz and rock—was out-of-sight. Gustavo and I danced from 10 till 2 without stopping practically. I felt so comfortable with him. He didn't come on to me. It was as if we were a couple of old friends hanging out together. He kept telling me how beautiful I looked. It's interesting how men react when I get all madeup. I never wear makeup to work, if I don't have to. I hate having to put that stuff on. It makes me feel like I have dirt on my face. But when I do people react as if I'm a totally different person, I love it. Gustavo is quite good-looking. Hair combed straight back. Slim nose. Full lips. He drives a Lincoln Continental, a Mark IV. He does very well selling commercial time for the station, makes the bucks. He owns a mansion in Pasadena. We'll probably go out again.

I'm curious if what they say about black men in bed is true. Will let you know (Ha Ha).

Love you, Laura

February 13, 1975
Santa Barbara

Dear Laura,

My father has cirrhosis of the liver. The doctor says not one more drop of alcohol. Can you believe it? I can't. I can't feel anything about this, but finally . . . finally.

Dad has started a little garden on the patio off the living room: tomatoes and herbs mostly. Mom is still at the bank. She says Dad can't really hold a job now due to his illness. He hasn't held a steady job in years! I think she used the same excuse in those days. Funny . . . life I mean.

I'm thinking seriously about going to UCSB so I can teach special ed. I like my job at Surface/Edge, but I want to do more than help run an office and I've got to distance myself from the halfway house. Possibly work with special ed kids. I don't know. I could start over the summer. I have an appointment to see a counselor in two weeks. Will keep you informed.

"Today is the first day of the rest of your life."
          Corita
Love always, Katharine

5/17/75

Dear Katharine,

I had to break it off with Gustavo. I mean he is just so fucking jealous all the time. God!! It's like every time I go out somewhere without him, even if it's just with a girlfriend from work, he fucking flips! I make it very clear from the start that I'm not interested in marriage (I was only interested in fucking his brains out actually).

I was working late last night. We had a show segment that I was helping prepare for our producer and I was the only person left in the office. I was supposed to I.D. some slides to give to the unit manager the next morning. I'd forgotten to do it and had to finish. There were over 200 to go through. It's around 8:00 p.m., there's nobody on the third floor but me and guess who walks in? Well, get this, Gustavo is standing there in the doorway and all of a sudden he unzips his pants and out flies his dick! I jumped out of my seat giggling with fear.

"Are you sure you want to say goodbye to him," he says with this bizarre smile on his face. Then he pulls me close—so roughly, it hurt! He demands to know who I think I am dumping him the way I did. Well, thank God, one of our local newsmen saunters in asking where the sales office is so he can check out the overnight ratings sheet. Gustavo left with him. I got the hell-out-of-there and ran to the parking lot and jumped in my car and headed home. I was scared, I mean really. Talk about crazy, Jesus! I thought he was going to hit me.

Gustavo found out I've been seeing one of the associate producers on the network's The Late Night Show. You know it airs at 1:00 a.m. with Raul Tyler interviewing some big name for an hour. Probably too late for you, but anyway his name is Tad McNeil and he is gorgeous and Gustavo saw us sitting together in the commissary this week having lunch so that probably pushed him over the edge. Maybe I should have been a nun!?

Love you very, Laura

P.S. How's your Dad doing?

October 27, 1973
Santa Barbara

Dear Laura,

The halfway house is gone. The funding ran out and David couldn't raise any more money. It was too much. I mean really and I couldn't keep up the bookkeeping and take classes at UCSB at night.

David is taking it hard. He believed in what he was doing and he did make a difference in some people's lives. I know he did and I told him so. He is depressed. Everyone involved is feeling broken and exhausted.

The good thing is that the four of us are going our separate ways. Emily has moved up to Oregon with a new boyfriend to build their own house from scratch. Shana and Steve are going to rent a small house of their own closer to her son's babysitter. David and I can't deal with Shana's drinking any longer, but Steve can and is trying to help her get sober again.

We are taking out a loan to buy a house of our own! Can you believe it? One of the former directors of the halfway house is an officer at the bank and said he would help us. David may even be starting a new business . . .his own auto repair shop. Cross your fingers.

"All things come in quiet silence."

Love always, Katharine

1/31/76

Dear Katharine,

I've been promoted to segment producer on the show!! I still haven't had time to absorb it yet. Amos, the one I was working with on that remote at the Chino Correctional Facility for Juveniles, had this offer to move to New York and take over a job in the network's entertainment division and had to leave on a Friday. He gave notice on the Monday before and we taped on the following Saturday. I produced the segment all by myself and Peter, our producer, said at the end of this month he would let me know about filling Amos's slot. He did yesterday and I am so jazzed!! Mom says it was meant to be, of course. I believe it.

I'll be researching the segments and lining up the remotes and writing the copy for the talent. Nancy Price is great to work with, she gets a little temperamental now and then, but we've never had any problems. She is pregnant and hasn't even told Peter yet, but she confided it to me.

This will mean even longer hours but I won't have a segment to produce every week, sometimes alternating weeks. My credit at the end of the show is not mixed in with all the other P.A.'s on the show, it's up there on its own slide. Showbiz is my life and I love it!!

It's just as well that Tad moved back to New York with Late Night. We only went out a few times and he turned out to be a real coke-head. Like he couldn't keep it up if you know what I mean. Mom always says, a man thinks from the waist down, well Tad failed—doing _and_ thinking.

No time for love (or sex) in my life now, just 70 to 80 hours a week on The Weekly Show. Today local public affairs, tomorrow maybe a network show, who knows?

I loved the pictures of your new house and it's great that David can run his shop out of the garage.

Love you, Laura

March 12, 1976

Dear Laura,

Thanks for bailing David and Steve out of jail. I told David I could have arranged for them to stay at my parents' place. Going to the mechanic's class in L.A. was important to him and since it was only overnight he insisted he would take care of it. When the policeman stopped to check them out while they were sleeping in his car, some outstanding tickets were discovered for both David and Steve...you know the rest. I'm enclosing a check to reimburse you for the $15.00. The guys didn't take much cash with them so that's why they couldn't pay the bail themselves. David wouldn't listen to me, as usual.

Love, Katharine

July 16, 1989
Vista del Mar Inn
Santa Barbara
2:46 p.m.

That check bounced, as I remember. I sent it back to Katharine in the mail and we never mentioned it again. I didn't care about the money; I was annoyed because David's pig-headedness led to the arrest. Everything about him annoyed me; my feelings were fueled by Katharine's complaints regarding his casual attitude about money and how much she worried about meeting their financial commitments. It seemed to me that she was unappreciated and her feelings dismissed. Yet she loved him and wanted to stay with him. Why?

Why did she have to get sick? Why did she have to go? Why do I feel like part of what makes me me, is missing? Why do I feel dead inside? Why can't I stop reading these letters? Why didn't I look at them before? Why was I so busy living a God damned life of sport-fucking that I never read through the lines? Why do I want to slit my wrists and follow her? To be with her, to not let her be alone there . . .

where she is. Why can't I leave here? Why don't I want to go back to my husband?

○

Katharine is calling me at the restaurant, and I have put her on hold twice now even though there are only a few customers in here today. This elderly couple sits quietly and eats their chicken salad, she drinks iced tea and he has an iced coffee, which he promptly spills. I have to clean it up as our bus boy got picked up by Immigration again and hasn't come back yet even though he promised he'd find a quick way. Depends on the *coyote*, said his mother when she called. Katharine waits on hold.

The couple pays their bill by leaving cash on the table as I'm washing out the mop. A $4 tip. Not bad for a lunch under $10. They must have felt guilty about the spill. I push the blinking phone light and Katharine tells me Sam Chase has written her a letter from Berkeley where he is still a freshman. He'd dropped out and is back for real now, supposedly.

She's happy that they still keep in touch once in a while. Sam wants to be a writer and Katharine, the avid reader, gives him lots of encouragement. He's in a philosophy class, she says, and for his final exam the instructor didn't hand any tests out, but wrote on the blackboard in large white chalk letters: WHY? That was it, simply WHY? He told them they had approximately an hour and fifteen minutes to complete the exam. Sam said the students all looked at each other like the professor was cracked and then proceeded to try to answer the perplexing question in their black-and-white comp books. Sam wrote fast and furiously, as did the others, beginning with *Webster's* definition of Why: *for what; for what reason, cause, or purpose?* He expounded at length on the whys of life, she said. He managed to fill up ten pages.

When the exams were handed back, Sam received a D, which floored him as he thought he had really aced it. Only one student in the class got an A. His answer was one word on one page. Katharine said Sam chased after him, when class was over, to see what that one-word answer could possibly be. The classmate showed Sam the one-word answer. On the paper the student had written BECAUSE.

Chapter Seven:
Floating

Laura Wells' Journal

July 16, 1989
Vista del Mar Inn
Santa Barbara
3:07 p.m.

The attendant, who turns out to be prematurely gray, has just brought me a club sandwich and a Bloody Mary, virgin, and left with a wink. Everything on the beach today feels virgin—my run on the sand to dive into a breaking wave was sudden, unfamiliar, and hard. The sand was searing hot, propelling me to sprint into the cool water. Waves swamped me down shore for an eternity, but in truth just minutes, and then it was all over—like losing my virginity.

Now I stir the red liquid with the celery and chomp down on the solid stick of green, which turns to mulch between my jaws. The crunch is ear-shattering. No one around me hears a thing. All movement slows. The silence is deafening. The waves roar, but I can't hear them. Their rhythm drives me to read, stop, start, read some more, wait, flow along on my own. Like each wave of the sea, I am propelled by its own rhythm. I see nothing but water, horizon, and sun shining into my plane of vision. An occasional sailboat or speedboat or airplane appears out there in the vast rich blueness of the sea and sky. I breathe in and people walk in slow motion. I breathe out and the sounds they make—their voices, their laughter, and the sonorous sounds of the sea—remain as they were. I'm more alive than I once was. I breathe in again, swallow, try to focus, and read:

11/16/76

Dear Katharine,

I'm still alive and life is hectic and crazy on the show. Yesterday the sales manager for the station did cartwheels down the hall, four of them right in a row, dressed in his suit and tie. I swear to God. He's having an affair with his cute little blonde secretary and he's a happy man.

You know how Mom is always saying, be independent, don't ever depend on a man, you don't need one. There's this guy who was working in production for a while and now works in the business office across the hall. He's really got my interest. He'd unit managed several of our remotes and we hit it off. Before that he was just a face I passed in the hall and smiled at. But working together such long hours gave me the opportunity to get to know him. I like him a lot. He's divorced, no kids. His name is John.

He's not my usual type. He's got thinning hair so he just shaves it all off. I love the sheen that bounces off his cue ball-bare head. He has a large handlebar mustache, wears aviator shaped glasses and is a bit overweight. He's very straight, never touched drugs in his life, but so funny and in-total-control. When we did remotes together everything went like clockwork. The engineering crew respected him as did everyone on our show. He kept his sense of humor no matter what happened. His favorite saying is, "I love a crisis!" and there is something very sexy about him. He's a big bear of a man with a power, yet a gentility that could take me in his arms and make everything right.

I don't know, Katharine, this feels, well, different . . . it must be the glasses.

Love, me

I blow the smoke out through my nostrils like I did as a smart-ass teen thinking how I looked so cool French inhaling. A young girl walking by on the boardwalk allowed me to bum a Tareyton Light off of her—tastes of smoking parchment. A cat nap made me groggy, and I hate that feeling in the middle of the day, especially when my past calls me to re-plough through it. The nicotine rush stopped an intense headache in its tracks.

Reading this letter, I remember how hard I fell for John. A casual work relationship or so I thought, but in John I found a lover who respected and cherished me—and not just for my looks or my body like the others. He was a man whose word was his bond. John's professionalism gained him much admiration and respect at the studio. He was promoted through the ranks into running our growing Production Department (then much later he took over the entire Finance division of the studio).

We had to be so careful not to reveal how infatuated we were with each other so he did not appear to favor me when handing out producing assignments of the many new shows we had in production. But there were complications which drove us apart for a time—

What's that noise . . . oh shit, "Hello!" I just barely pick up the phone inside the room on the last ring. I don't know why I ran so fast. Maybe I thought it was Katharine calling but . . .

"Oye, mija, donde estas?"

"Mom, I'm here in Santa Barbara, don't you remember? I told you." I really didn't; Ana told her, but what does it matter. I try to camouflage my disappointment that it's just Mom. Katharine's voice is the sound I wanted to hear just now.

"Laura, are you still seeing that person, John?" How odd. I wonder why she asks me this, in this way, just now. "Sí Mom, we still are." I figure that's the best answer for now as anything further and she'll be lost.

"Oye, why are you with him?" Funny, I'm wondering the same thing. "I can't believe you'd really sleep with that!"

"Mom, let me speak to Ana, please." I've learned that these odd segues of Mom's are best ignored. No sense in reasoning her out of her warped labyrinth of reality. That is the very same thing she said to me when I told her I was in love with my boss, John, all those years ago. She had met him a couple of times when she came to have lunch with me in those days and found him unattractive, uninteresting, and way too conservative to be trifled with.

"Mrs. Laura, your mama, she is getting *más loca*." Ana explains how Mom refuses to put her clothes on these last few days, and often Ana discovers her sitting on the kitchen counter stark naked in the middle of the night while snacking on a croissant. Then Mom ends up burning herself with the spilled coffee she insists on dunking a croissant into and makes a mess of the place. I assure Ana if she can just hang on another few days I will be back and will hire more help. She balks and I offer to double her salary. John won't appreciate that, but I will convince him of the necessity later. I don't know what else to do at this point . . .

The waves cover my ankles as I walk up the beach. I have to walk—have to get away from that room, that phone, those voices, and that prison in that past present.

I sit down on a white sand slope just above the waterline and watch two little girls build a sand castle. One with black curls flying, looking about five, runs back and forth between the construction site and the water's edge, determined to fill her plastic blue buckets. The older one with ebony bangs and bun falling out, maybe nine, points to where to fill the sand ruts to make a moat and where to pile on more sand to increase the heights of the drip turrets she is designing. They work in tandem and their movements mimic the back-and-forth motion of the waves. Their mother beckons them over to her to dry off as she is packing up their things to leave. The girls ignore her at first, too focused on the landscape of their innocence to leave. But soon they leave off, join their mother and depart . . . as soon too, so must I.

The sun warms my back as I brush off my sandy feet and return to my room. That parade of people and things past that pluck at me, insisting I read them in a whole new way. And so I do.

January 13, 1977

Dear Laura,

I'm sorry you stopped seeing John. I thought things were going so well and right before Christmas, too.

School and work are still keeping me incredibly busy and...I've met someone, his name is Sean, in one of my classes. Younger by six years and 6'2". We have struck up a friendship...more than that actually. Last Tuesday night we decided to go for coffee after class. We left early. I didn't leave his apartment until after 11. Fortunately David was asleep when I got home. I did tell him, in the morning, a group of us went out together after class and he accepted that.

I mean I know Sean is a boy, but not in bed. I felt like the "older woman" in control and together for once. Don't ask me why or how it happened, it just did. Not seeing him over the holidays made me miss him so.

Things with David—so tense. He's working hard and I've been doing the books for the shop and as usual we fight about money. He wants to buy more equipment. I think we ought to save to pay our taxes, instead of taking out a loan or being late and having the IRS on our backs.

Laura, I had the strangest dream that you came and told me you were pregnant and that you weren't going to keep it. Is everything all right?

"Flowers grow out of the darkness." Corita
Love always, Katharine

5/10/77

My dear Katharine,
I still think you did the right thing. It's just as well that Sean took a teaching job out of state. If he sends you flowers every so often, God, isn't that a sort of rave review?

Dropping out of school was a tough decision and I know leaving Surface/Edge was a big step also, but with you working at the shop fulltime, David will feel more supported by you _and_ you can keep an eye on things by keeping expenses from getting out of hand.

I really thought John and I would never get back together. Who would have thought that the first time we sleep together I get pregnant!

When that girl moved in with him right after, I was devastated. He did warn me that she was going to even before we started getting involved, but still... When she left after a month—did I play hard to get? I ran back to him. Having to see each other at work was pure hell while we were apart and I have no pride where this man is concerned. He went with me to the clinic, paid for it, took care of me and held me in his arms the whole night while I cried. I fell head-over-heels in love with him then.

He offered to marry me, but I couldn't. I'd always feel that he married me to "make an honest woman" out of me, not because he loved me. He once said he could never imagine cheating on a spouse and truly has disdain for most of the people here that do and believe me, everyone here does. I'm completely smitten with his sense of honor.

Slight problem is he's a terrible dresser. He wears these horrid polyester suits and I'm hoping to change that ASAP. He could be very big in this company if he chose to and I feel I can give him the little polish he needs to make it. God I sound like a wife already!

Love you, Laura

P.S. Mom doesn't approve, of course.

I lay down the letters, not neatly, I let them fall from my hands. I must remember to return them to their proper piles; Katharine's Life and Laura's Life. I must remember to place them face down and keep a sense of chronology. I must.

It's late afternoon, or is it early evening? I'm not certain and I don't care. Casey Jones will be by soon, dropping off its commuters and signaling hello-goodbye with a loud whoo-whoo. A frequent sound I've become accustomed to not hearing. I walk back out onto the patio of my room and sit to stare at the jacaranda trees. The lavenders have faded, but the trees retain their beauty, each like a ball gown hanging dormant until next year's gala. They dance and sway to the tune of the rustling leaves.

Having to terminate that pregnancy all those years ago still brings tears. The pain of that decision is still engraved within my hurt cells. Katharine's pain leading to an affair with Sean and others later, but still continuing with an unappreciative David, was real, and yet she just skimmed over it, like she did all of her other hurts. The letters were just the bare surface of the volcano underneath.

○

I'm sitting in the commissary of the studio having lunch with one of John's oldest and closest friends, Jeremiah. He and other people around the station notice that John and I are a "campus couple" as he likes to refer to all the couples who couple in this place. Jeremiah doesn't necessarily approve of me, I think. He feels that John will get hurt because of my past history. John says they both thought of me as a sort of bubble-gummer with a string of boyfriends. Jeremiah shares this opinion, even though he's a unit manager and we have worked together and get along rather pleasantly. Jeremiah is telling me:

"Do you realize how important children are to John?" I don't remember how we get onto this subject. He continues:

"John will make a great parent because he's a kid himself." Jeremiah reminds me about his own two boys and how John loves to play with them when he comes over. Jeremiah says he'll spend hours throwing ball with them in the backyard or wrestling with them on the lawn.

"When John was married to Cheryl, probably one of the big reasons they split up was because she didn't want children, and later she found out she couldn't have them." There is some moral to this story that Jeremiah is telling me, I'm sure of it. I already know some of the story from John. Jeremiah is trying to warn me that John is a serious person, not someone to be trifled with.

"John was trying to convince Cheryl that it could work out even if they adopted, but she finally told him she didn't want kids and didn't want to be married either. After they broke up John was pretty down for a long time."

What Jeremiah doesn't know is that it's barely two weeks since my abortion. Two weeks since we terminated John's heart's desire. Two weeks since I realized I can't live without him. Two weeks since I ended his dream. As Jeremiah is talking to me tears stream down my face. I try to wipe them away with the soft white napkins they give us in this place.

The commissary is full of employees both from the network and the station. The voices are loud, blending into one big buzz like a thousand bees buzzing at once. Celebrities wander in and sit in The Blue Room, the private waited area. I think I see Cher and, yes, isn't that what's-his-name?

Tears still roll down my chin. The more I try to suppress them the more they refuse to stop. I see Jeremiah seeing me, seeing him seeing my wetness and my redness and he does not outwardly acknowledge anything is wrong. Two tables away, Peter, my boss, eyes me with concern on his face. Finally all I hear Jeremiah saying is, "Do you realize how much John wants a child?" The words *wants a child* echo in my head, I can't stop the words, *wants a child*, and I can't stop the crying. I get up to leave, the room spins, the people blur . . . and everything goes blue.

I wake up in the health office right around the corner from the commissary. I'm lying on a brown leather sofa staring up at a white acoustic ceiling. A fluorescent light is staring back at me. Did whoever carry me here feel like my 105 pounds weighed a lot, I wonder. I hear Jeremiah asking the nurse, "Will she be all right?"

"I think so, she probably had a dizzy spell," the nurse answers.

I wonder what happened. The last thing I remember is seeing blue. Blue is for a boy, isn't it? When they give you a baby boy in the hospital don't they wrap it in blue?

O

Standing out on the hotel patio, I walk over to the table to finish my cold cup of coffee and brownie (a sugar rush always helps), but the sea gulls have beat me to the brownie—and the coffee tastes as bad as it looks. The attendant asks me if I'm done. Not yet, I say, I need a drink—a real one.

I see an elderly couple walk by in the parking lot. By the look of them I would guess them to be in their seventies. He is wearing a polo shirt in red and she is wearing a matching one. They both have on white bottoms: he, slacks, and her, a skirt. They both have matching white hair, and she is wearing a white sun visor with Fila on the bill. They walk tall and straight, not bent over. She is slightly shorter than he. They hold hands. They look toward me in my flowered silk cover-up and they nod. I nod back.

Katharine will never know this feeling of quiet familiarity and companionship with a lifetime mate, nor will she see her daughter grow old. She will never again be able to comfort Jillian when she cries, hold her close when she is frightened, or watch her walk down the aisle to an anxious groom or see her own grandchildren. I will never see my grandchildren either.

Can John and I ever enjoy the quiet repose that propinquity brings? I never imagined at one time I could live without him. Now I don't want . . . to go on living . . .with him. Have we grown too far apart and hurt each other too much?

Katharine proved she couldn't survive without David. If they had never broken up, would she still be here today? This question plagues me and repeats itself over and over. The letters hold many questions and many answers; I must keep on reading and searching.

I'm amazed we saved as many letters as we did. I remember there being many, many more; all the notes passed in class, left in each other's locker, or hidden in our luggage as a surprise after our overnights, then the joy of finding a letter inside my bag after a reluctant farewell, return home, and unpacking. We both loved the game we played of pretending she or I wasn't stuffing a letter in the other's bag. After Katharine moved to another school we corresponded weekly. Once she moved to Santa Barbara we called and still wrote monthly. Once she became severely depressed, the letters dwindled. But that was much later.

○

"I decided to throw some of the old correspondence out; it's the past and I needed to let it go," Katharine says.

We've been talking for about forty-five minutes because she keeps putting me on hold, fielding customer service calls and calling in orders for auto parts.

It's Saturday afternoon around 2 o'clock, and I'm still in bed. We've taped past midnight for the last three nights in a row. Last night the guest for my segment didn't show so I had to madly re-write copy for our host; but he loves to ad-lib and hardly used any of it. Showbiz?! I came home so wired I couldn't get to sleep until 3 a.m., partly due to Mom's loud snoring. I could hear her even with my door shut. Katharine commented on it once, after she'd spent a night with me at home during high school. She couldn't sleep because of her dream: a judge was giving a verdict in a courtroom and when the judge opened his mouth to speak, the sound that came out was my mother's snoring. Mom's snoring was definitely a test of friendship.

My left ear is getting numb so I switch the receiver to my right ear. I've decided to stay in bed all day.

"Yeah, I threw out a bunch of that stuff too, right after Mom and I moved in here. I didn't feel like dealing with all of it. There were so many boxes to unpack, you know," I say, hoping I won't regret this decision some day. "There are other boxes and they're still in the garage. I'll have to deal with them some day, but not today." I laugh after this last line as a bomb wouldn't get me out of this bed.

"Laura, the other phone is ringing and I've got a customer waiting for his bill and David needs something. I really should go, okay." Her tone shows she's hassled, yet she always puts her good-byes in such a way, as if she's afraid to hurt my feelings because she's the first one to say good-bye.

"Good to hear your voice, write soon, bye," I say, hating to hang up. Talking to Katharine makes me feel connected, somehow; like plugging in to humanity itself.

O

It's 6:15. I reach for the hotel phone. Should I call David? I have such a hard time with that thought. His presence stirs up so many divergent feelings in me: anger, resentment, empathy, understanding, and pity. I thought I had worked them out, but now I'm not so sure. I want to finish the letters first. I'm afraid if I ask him about Katharine's girlhood molestation he will take her letters away from me and that would be like taking away my reason for being right now.

David knows where I am and he hasn't called me. I let the thought go for the time being.

I need to call Sherry at Outside/Inside. She's probably furious with me. I submitted the stories so long ago, four months was it, or last month? That's all so far away. Time present beckons, and demands, and I just run from it. Don't want to think about anything but where I left off. The remnants of two lives lie in front of me. I reach down to neaten the letters I dropped and replace them in their proper piles, then pick fresh from these mesmerizing souvenirs of time past.

September 30, 1977

Dear Laura,

How do you like your new address? Your Mom will get used to it. John's house sounds wonderful and is not that far from your Mom's place is it?

I'll be down before Christmas. Mom is doing her guilt thing again: why don't I call her more, why don't I visit more often? Funny how she always has an excuse for not coming up to see _me_. "Can't leave your father," she says.

I'd rather not stay with them, so maybe I can impose on you? David doesn't really like me to leave.

Shana has started working for us in the office and it's helping take some of the pressure off of me. It's the one eight-hour time period she isn't drunk. Her son is developing a lot slower than the other kids in daycare. I wonder if Shana poisoned him with alcohol when she was carrying him. Steve is so good with little Trevor, treats him like a son. Steve's turning out to be one of our best mechanics. Luckily his paycheck didn't bounce ... this week. Had lunch yesterday with Evelyn, remember I told you we worked together at Surface/Edge. She showed up with a note for me from Sean. It's been so hard. She's the only one up here that knows about him. I miss Sean, but he's happy with his teaching job and ...

"Some people see things and say why
I dream of things that never were and
say why not." G.B. Shaw

Love, Katharine

2/18/78

Dear Katharine,

I felt so much better after we hung up last night. You're right,
if it's going to happen it will. It's just that I've never loved anyone
like I love John before. I think I wanted to marry him from the
beginning. He is so ethical and high-principled. I really admire
and respect him.

Everyone at work knows we live together, even the higher level
executives at work treat me differently since they found out. I
want to stay with him for the rest of my life.

You said be open and honest with my feelings and I have been,
but he's holding back. We do get along better now and a lot of our
fighting has stopped since I moved in.

Mother is still being so difficult. It's as if she expected me to
stay with her forever and never have a life of my own. I feel a lot of
the reason John and I fought was because of her interference. She
lays on the guilt if I don't call her every day. She refuses to break
the umbilical cord and I'm nearly 27. She just never expected me
to pick a man like John. God, Katharine, what's happened to me?
I've fallen in love with a Republican!

Lately we've hardly seen each other with the horrendous hours
we're working. His department is going through a computer
conversion and since becoming a producer my work has been a
killer. I'm falling asleep as I write this. Time to run and get a cup

of the Drano they call coffee in the commissary. Thanks again for being there.

Love you lots,

Laura

P.S. John said, "Katharine's very special and a true friend to you." Haven't you always been?

Laura Wells
&
John Newton
are tying the knot.
Please join us in celebration
September 9, 1978
at Twelve O'Clock Noon.
Newton Residence
301 Petit Avenue
Studio City, California
R.S.V.P.
Buffet Lunch

October 7, 1978

Dear Laura,

Lake Tahoe sounds like a beautiful place for a honeymoon, maybe someday David and I will go, who knows? I don't know anymore.

The business is up and down. Money is so tight. I'm thinking of going back to my old job or finding a new one or... I don't know. That seems to be a recurring phrase with me of late. David and I are still fighting about money. He wants to expand and buy more equipment. The backyard looks like a garden of abandoned cars.

How I would love to have a little flower garden and add a second story to the house so we could have our bedroom upstairs! The thought of spending more money makes me nervous. We don't have it and David won't believe me. It's the same old argument. Thank you, again, for letting us stay with you. The reception was really something, Laura, with all those umbrella tables and so many people!

It was interesting seeing Joy Chan again. She was so distant and treated me like an acquaintance she hardly remembered. David thought she was a snob and wondered how I could ever have considered her a friend. Funny isn't it, how things change.

David and I have been talking about marriage since yours. The idea of signing a marriage paper freaks him and he can't bring himself to do it. but he says he'd like to have a child.

The phones are ringing. I must close.

"Lovers alone wear the sunshine."

e.e. cummings

Love always, Katharine

12/20/78

Katharine dear,

Again, I'm so sorry to hear that your Mom isn't feeling well. I thought the doctor told her to quit smoking? My mom never listens to her doctor either. Your dad sounds like he's holding up. I sent your Mom a get well-card from my mother and myself.

Work has finally slowed down, it usually does around the holidays. We shot our Xmas show at the Old Mission Inn in Riverside on November 30 and New Years was taped December

15th so I've got a few minutes to breathe. I was able to get our cards out before Xmas this year!

My thoughts are with you, dearest.

Love,

Laura

P.S. John sends his best.

Service of Memory

For

Betty Iris Taylor

Born	May 7, 1912
Passed away	March 5, 1979 Tarzana
Service held	March 17, 1979 2:00 p.m.
At the	Old South Church
Service conducted by	The Reverend Frank English
Funeral Director	Fireside Greens, Granada Hills

Service of Memory

For

Lawrence Gregory Taylor

Born	August 15, 1920
Passed away	March 6, 1979 North Hollywood
Service held	March 17, 1979 2:00 p.m.
At the	Old South Church
Service conducted by	The Reverend Frank English
Funeral Director	Fireside Greens, Granada Hills

April 28, 1979

Dear Laura,

It's been so hard trying to get the apartment emptied out and the estate settled. There was some money in Mom's bank account almost $10,000. Mom must have been saving for years and never said a word. Many of Mom's clothes, her aunt wanted and Dad's brother didn't want any of his clothes so the Salvation Army took the rest.

Once the apartment was empty the brownness of the walls from years of cigarette smoke stood out like headlights alongside my memories: all stained.

It's true Dad couldn't survive without her. They figure he died a few hours after the hospital called to tell him of Mom's final heart attack. Ironic isn't it. I thought the drinking would kill him all along. A broken heart, my father? They said natural causes, but it's all so different than I imagined it would be. So many things unresolved, unsaid, not done ... I feel a weight lifting. I don't know. There's that phrase again.

Thanks again for the beautiful flowers. No, I haven't had a chance to look in any of those old boxes yet ... later ... I can't right now. Thank your mom for her kind words, also.

"There is no birth of consciousness without pain." Jung
Love always, Katharine

7/3/79

Dear Katharine,
Mother is going into the hospital for surgery. She's had some problems for a long while and refused to get to the doctor about it. It's her brain and the possibility of a tumor. I hope to God not and am putting her in God's hands. Say a prayer for her. Will call you as soon as I know.
Love, me

P.S. It must be my turn.

Chapter Eight:
Hunger

Laura Wells' Journal

July 16, 1989
Vista del Mar Inn
Santa Barbara
A Minute to Midnight

In the middle of my third drink at the hotel bar, I walk out with the last Irish coffee submerged inside my purse with the short red sipper straw sticking out of it and head down to the boardwalk to sit on one of the damp, dark gray benches to listen. The waves break lazily on the beach below. The breeze is soft and soothing. The hotel floodlights brighten the foam-filled swirls left by the receding waves. My thoughts are like those swirls, curved in places and incomplete without closure. Seaweed floats in circles, interrupting the foamy shapes. The kelp glistens in small little piles, some stringy and stretched out like long freshly washed hair, others a blur of tangles half buried in the wet sand. The tide comes in and wipes their imprints clean, if only for a moment. With the next wave, patterns begin to form themselves anew, then are wiped away, and so with the next wave, and the next. The patterns in the sand aren't the only things that are wiped out. I feel wiped myself and return to my room.

I'm sprawled across the bed closest to the window, and arrayed on the floor are the letters surrounding me like a moat around a castle. It's dark except for the nightstand light that casts a yellow hue in the room and onto this page. The shadows of my hand follow me with every right-directed movement. I should feel sleepier, drunker, but my thoughts continue to ebb and flow like the waves. I wanted to leave them behind, just for a while, but like the distant sound of the ocean my memories have followed me to my room. There's no escape from the past—such as from the time John preferred living in sin to marrying me.

○

"Don't push him, Laura, he'll marry you if you let things be," Katharine says. Why is it so easy for her to give me advice and so hard for her to follow mine?

"Now you sound like me," I say.

"Well, we've been friends for fifteen years, so I suppose we may rub off on each other now and then."

It's late; John isn't home from work yet and David is at a karate class, so Katharine and I can talk on the phone freely and uninterrupted. She always keeps track of how many years we've been friends, right down to the minute. I never do, and when she says how long it has been it's always such a surprise.

"Laura, it's been five years, five months, seven days, two minutes, three seconds."

"Laura, it's been ten years, six months, twelve days."

"Laura, it's been thirteen years, two months, nine days and fifteen minutes."

She has always marked our relationship with the passing of time. I choose to assume that we'll be friends for the whole of our lives. I cannot imagine my life without Katharine at the other end of the phone or a postage stamp away in Santa Barbara. Our union cannot be defined by the mundane-ness of days, months, or years. For me we are timeless friends.

"Why am I acting this way? Usually it's me that's being chased, but with John all I think of is wedding bells and being barefoot and pregnant, God I'm hopeless," I whine; but it's the truth.

"This is the first time you've offered your heart, Laura." I know she's right. I've practically proposed to him. This isn't my style.

When I moved out of Mom's house, I did it while she was at work. I knew she would leave early as Saturdays were her busiest days. I didn't give her any advance warning. I emptied my room out and took everything else that was mine, even stuff out of the garage. I borrowed John's four-wheel-drive jeep and loaded it to the top of the back window. When I arrived at John's, before I unloaded a thing, I called her at the restaurant and said,

"Mom, I've moved in with John." There was a big sigh and then,

"Okay, *mija*, but it's going to be hard to pay for the house all by myself." Whenever she needed money she always seemed to have it, yet she was so good at crying poor.

"I'll still help out for a while," I assured her, but I was lying and didn't. I was so glad to be out from under her manipulation-by-guilt approach to parenting. I think the last straw was when she started lecturing me about coming in late on work nights from seeing John as if I were a sophomore in high school. I was in my mid-twenties.

"Actually," I remind Katharine, "John says he'll marry me when I get my American Express bill paid off." John makes me laugh. My spending makes him nervous. He makes this crack about my American Express bill all the time.

"If you love him enough, *you'll* pay it off," Katharine says. We both laugh a little more. John walks into the bedroom greeting me, and I tell Katharine I have to go and hang up. He collapses on the bed next to me and we put our arms around each other, and he says,

"What a day! I need a foot rub." I give great foot, John likes to tell me.

"Who was on the phone?" he asks, while I rub lotion into his sore heel and around the ball of his left foot.

"Katharine," I answer.

"Oh yeah, what's up? Ouch!" I just hit a knot of taut muscles and am manipulating them hard to release the tension in his arch.

"Not much," I say as he flinches. "I was just telling her how I'm close to paying off my American Express bill."

July 17, 1989
Vista del Mar Inn
Santa Barbara
6:22 a.m.

I awake to hear the brandy glass fall onto the carpet. The funeral announcement card is stuck to the side of my head. Slept right through Casey Jones. God, what a headache—like a hammer hitting an anvil. I think I stopped counting after drink number five. Think I'll skip breakfast.

I also forgot to close the blinds and the sun is blaring yellow, white and orange at me through the bedroom windows. I drop my chin over the edge of the bed and squint down to see blurs of handwritten and typewritten pages underneath my fallen glass. The glass has a small residue of brandy that has spilled onto a letter. I snatch it up and wipe the spot of brown liquid away. None of the writing is obscured. The taste of morning mouth forces me into the bathroom to brush my teeth. When I glance into the dressing table mirror I realize I've slept in my clothes. A shower is what I need. I want to feel the stinging heat of that water. I want to feel fresh and new. While the beads of water splay onto my body, I recall my dream.

Katharine and I are together. We're trying to talk, but we keep getting interrupted by the sound of a phone ringing. The picture changes; she's lying down and her feet are in my lap. I'm massaging them. Some people enter the room, I don't recognize them. The picture changes again and instead of massaging her feet, I'm kissing her feet in a very matter-of-fact way as we are about to get into a warm bathtub together. I tell her everything will be okay. She smiles hesitantly. Again we're interrupted by shadows of vague people entering the room, calling our attention away from one another. Men I don't recognize. The dream ends.

Dwelling on this dream I feel the heated water so soothing, so stimulating that I begin to rub my right hand between my legs—back and forth. With my left hand I rub the white soap bar marked Ivory over both of my breasts. They feel like satin and the nipples harden to my touch. I'm breathing harder and faster as my fingers do the work, massaging the small bud of my clitoris vigorously. I lie down in the tub and the water feels hotter as I spread my legs. I'm compelled to open them as wide as I can and plunge my first two fingers in deeper and deeper so that I can feel my cervix. I imagine Katharine is with me in the tub and we are finishing what we couldn't in the dream. I let out a cry as the contractions of my uterus begin—wave upon wave breaks upon my reddened body. Lying there drenched from the steady stream of hot water, exhausted from the intensity of the coming—the tears come, then the sobs come. The sounds they make echo in the bathroom, and sound somewhat like those of two people crying.

Looking again into the mirror of the small dressing room just outside the bathroom, I see myself wrapped in a dove grey bath sheet. The tears have not stopped flowing. My whole body flows wet, and I can't tell the difference between the cleansing water and the cleansing tears.

Sitting at the glass table with only the sound of the overhead caned-wood fan blades cutting the quickly diminishing cool morning air, I've put the next group of letters in order. I remember to keep the Katharine Pile and the Laura Pile separate. Mustn't mix them up. I want to read them in the proper order, otherwise they'll blend together and become one blur of two lives, and for that I'm not ready. The decaf minus my usual splash of half-and-half bluffs me into feeling more awake than I am. I'm hoping 3% caffeine will be enough. The piles of letters draw me like something forbidden. I'm obliged by the old that is new again that they continue to present me and I can't rest until the journey is complete. I pour another cup of coffee and glance outside. No clouds. It's going to be another beautiful day of hot California summer weather and I don't care. I care about the weather inside this room, inside of me. I take a nibble of last night's leftover hardened whole-wheat dinner roll dragged off of somebody else's table on the way to my room and wash it down with a sip of coffee, and read.

December 29, 1980
Santa Barbara

Dear Laura,

How soon is help moving in for your mom? At least she hasn't wandered away? Does she even remember me? I can remember when I first stayed over at your house in Hollywood during junior high, how she let us stay up late watching old movies on your black and white set. I kept waiting for someone to yell at us to get to bed and no one did. Funny how she would sit with us and watch and laugh and giggle. She loves life and she loves you. I know you've had your battles. I witnessed many of them, but I can never forget when we were in 11th grade: how she drove us around one Friday night in her restaurant delivery truck (using a screw driver to shift gears because the column shift lever had broken off) so we could

143

toilet paper your boyfriend's house (what was his name? Tony). Do you recall when he and his brothers doused us with water balloons? Your mom chased after them instead of running away screaming, like we did. We were cowards, but your mom was really something. I love her and I love you, Laura dear. Give yourself time. I am.

"The dark has its own light." Roethke
Katharine

3/1/81

Dear Katharine,

John and I've decided to try for a baby, seriously. I've gone off the pill. Thrown caution to the wind.

I hate working in television. I never realized how much—until after mother became ill. Peter, now our Executive Producer, was very understanding about giving me all that time off. It's just that I don't feel like "showbiz" is part of me any more—getting up at 4 in the morning in preparation for some inane remote at a golf course, a rodeo, a local college, or video-taping talking heads and dealing with way too much prima donna talent. There's a hell of a lot more to life than news, weather and sports!

I want a stab at domesticity, something Mother always warned me to stay away from. The old be-independent, be-a-businesswoman speech. Now that she's losing her own reality this dims in my memory. Yet why do I feel like she would think of me as giving in by admitting that I want a child and want to be dependent on John? What's the answer?

We've had to sell some of Mom's antiques as her care is costing!! My aunt didn't want anything but a few old photographs of herself and Mom when they were kids. Remember Sylvia? Mom's sister's wicked stepdaughter who began her groupie career when she fucked that musician in the Monkees. She appeared insisting that Mom had left her a hand-carved Chinese ivory vase (an old wedding present). Mom let her take it. Sylvia

144

is moving to England to live with some record producer. Would you believe that Mom was loaning Sylvia money, even though she still had her drug problem. I found the cancelled checks. Mom could never let go of her. I'll bet the bitch pawned the vase.

Love to you, Laura

July 17, 1981

Dear Laura,

Congratulations again! I am so happy for you. Your February 28 due date was Sam Chase's birthday. Remember he broke up with me after his prom because I refused to smoke grass and sleep with him. The sixties never did end for him. They never really started for me.

You two didn't take long. Now David is pressuring me about a baby. I've put him off for almost four years and, well, I've had my IUD removed so...

I am too overwhelmed by the whole process of a child and insecure about the kind of parent I will make. My childhood was not an example I want to follow. It has been over two years since Mom and Dad died and I feel like there was so much to say that was never said.

I am plagued by a recurring dream about them: Dad is standing in the kitchen pouring himself a drink, sneering at me. I try to stab him with the kitchen knife Mom is using to slice a steak, but I can not grasp it. Every time I reach for it, it disappears. Mom sees what I am about to do and does nothing. The dream ends before I reach Dad. I have this *dream over and over again. David shook me out of it the last time because my cries kept him awake. I have thought about seeing a psychiatrist, but we do not have insurance. Money is a problem as usual. I don't know. Looks like I need some answers of my own.*

"Flowers grow out of dark moments." Corita

Katharine

10/31/81

Dear Katharine,
I can't believe how hectic work has been. I've been feeling so well and now all of a sudden I'm having swelling in my ankles. The doctor says I need to rest more. I say I will, but I don't. I eat like a pig all the time—hamburgers, French fries, chocolate shakes, raisin bagels with cream cheese. Usually I'm in the middle of taping, tied up in editing, writing copy, or surveying new locations so I don't eat what I should. That's when our unit manager says, "It's okay, you're eating for two now."

Today we taped our Halloween show and the whole crew showed up in costume. Our director wore his boxer shorts, with little pumpkin designs, outside of his jeans and brought a can of Lysol that he sprays during tapings when the control room gets too thick with smoke—Thank God! I came as a pregnant lady of course. Everyone wanted to know if I was carrying a bowling ball. I'm huge. It's funny how different friends at the station like to touch my growing belly all the time. As if by doing so they snatch a spark of energy from the budding life inside of me.

Tonight John and I handed out candy to the trick-or-treaters—they looked so adorable! Kids dressed in pirate costumes, hobo costumes, gypsies and princesses, Darth Vaders, etc. The youngest ones, two and three-years-old, looked the sweetest as they toddled up our brick front porch steps for their M&Ms and squeaking out Thank You in their tiny voices. We realized that next Halloween we'd have a little trick-or-treater of our own.

When I told John that I wasn't going back to work after the baby's born, his response was,

"You realize, of course, our income will be cut in half."

I told him I didn't care. I want to raise our baby, not have some illegal alien do it for us. One of the other Associate Producers I work with came back to work six weeks after her baby was born and hardly sees her daughter. These sixty-to-seventy-hour weeks would definitely keep me away from our baby too. I want to breast-feed. I can't imagine leaving the baby with a stranger. I missed my last doctor appointment and couldn't get back in to see him for another three weeks. Thank God "showbiz-is-my-life" for only a few more months. I'm so happy.

Love you, Laura

December 29, 1987

Dear Laura,

Thank you for the beautiful baby roses. Is pink a hint? David is walking on air. He received the call about my pregnancy test before I did. When I came home from the market he said we needed to go out shopping right away as we were having a new guest who would be staying permanently. I thought he had drunk one too many beers, because shopping is something we can not afford to do. He then announces,

"We are having a baby!" and put his arms around me and held me. I have been walking around in a daze ever since. I do not feel like anything is growing, yet I know there is.

I hope you are listening to your doctor now and resting as much as possible. You could not keep the same pace as before, you knew that. I am sorry about your swelling. Please take care. And, yes, I will come down for the shower next month. Thanks for the invitation.

"You bring the spring." Corita

Love always, Katharine

Laura Wells' Journal

July 17, 1989
Vista del Mar Inn
Santa Barbara
11:00 a.m.

I put the letters down. I can't go on with this, not right now. I can't. I need a moment. I know what's going to happen; I know what lies within the next sheets of paper. It's been seven years that I never held that little piece of life in my hands. I've buried the loss and, damn you Katharine, you've brought it all back. Why did we keep these letters? Why did you have to die? Why did you get to keep your daughter only to reject her in the end? Why did I have to read these goddamn fucking letters? I can't write anymore, I can't see anymore because here they come again, these memories that won't leave me alone.

O

We're driving to the hospital, my mother-in-law and I. She is lost and I'm screaming at her from the back seat of her Mercedes.

"Angie, hurry, the contractions are so hard I think it's coming—"

"I'm sorry, I made a wrong turn. It will be okay if I can turn left up ahead and—"

"Oh GOD, I don't know if I can hold on much longer, oh my God please let Dr. Felix be waiting for me!" I'm only eight months. This isn't supposed to happen yet, not yet. John's been called away on a last-minute trip to New York. This wasn't supposed to be like this. He's supposed to be with me!

"Hold on, we're almost there, that's it, straight up on the right," Angie says in a relieved and reassuring voice. All I can do is scream. I feel like I'm about to explode. The contractions are so close together, so intense, I can barely take a breath. I still have more Lamaze classes to go. I haven't learned everything yet.

"I feel like pushing, the baby's coming," I shriek out of control.

Someone lifts me into a wheelchair and they're pushing me through the hospital doors onto the elevator. Before it closes I yell to whomever will listen, "Call John, he's got to come home, NOW!"

As the attendant rolls me onto the maternity ward, a nurse comes over to me and says,

"Blow out the candle, breathe like this." She blows with pursed lips, her face nose to nose with mine until I do as she says. I'm being lifted onto a table; the nurse asks me if I can walk.

"I can't even stand up," I say.

I don't know how, but I've been changed into a gown and put on a table with stirrups. Dr. Felix is there, behind his green mask. I can hear his soft and calming voice intoning

"That's it, Laura, push, it will be okay, that's it."

I hear him and I see him, but I feel like I'm somewhere else, watching from outside of myself. I feel my body controlling me, not my mind, and I must submit to its will. I push, and fluid gushes out of me like a waterfall.

"The head's out, Laura, now push a little more."

I give a final exhausting push and . . . it's a girl! A whole human being has just rocketed out of me, a glimpse of greenish-blue; but shouldn't she be reddish-purple? Dr. Felix is suctioning the baby—my baby. She doesn't make a sound. I fall back exhausted on the table. I feel like I've just played at the Super Bowl with no time-outs and no substitutions.

"Ohhh, she's too small," I hear one of the nurses say.

"She's not breathing," says another.

They whisk the baby away to another part of the room where I can't see her.

"Dr. Felix, what is it, what's happened?" I hear myself plead, "Please, somebody?" Then another doctor puts a black mask over my face. I try to push it away as he says in an irritated voice, "Hey lady, it's not my fault you're here."

Someone holds down my hands. In an instant I see blackness, hear nothingness.

I open my eyes to see Dr. Felix standing over me; his mask is off. I can see his graying mustache and beard. I wish his face would stop spinning around in circles. It feels like years have passed since I last saw him. He reminds me of Bilbo Baggins. He says my name in that gentle bedside manner of his.

"Laura, dear, how are you feeling?"

"Like a space cadet," I mumble.

"Your mother-in-law reached John and he's on his way home. Oh Laura, I'm sorry, I told you it would be okay, I'm so sorry."

"Where's my baby, Dr. Felix, where is she?" I'm afraid of the answer.

"She didn't make it, honey."

I know this already, deep down inside I know. I remember the words, "...she isn't breathing." Tears roll down my cheeks as Dr. Felix explains to me why her life lasted barely two minutes outside my womb. The words are a blur, something about aspirating meconium. When my water broke it resembled pea soup, he says.

I can't listen any longer, don't want to be here any longer, get me out of here, I think to myself. Angie appears and grabs hold of my hand. She smells of many Winstons. I look at her, but can't speak. "I know," she says quietly, her voice breaking, "I know, dear." Just before I lose consciousness, I hear a voice say, "I wish I were dead, I wish . . . I were . . . dead."

◯

July 17, 1989
Vista del Mar Inn
Santa Barbara
11:18 a.m.

I look down at my lap. Katharine's letter is tear-stained and some of the royal blue ink lines have been smudged. I grab for a tissue, blow my nose, wipe my eyes, and dab at the smudges. They hold fast and my attempts fail to put them right. There they stay. Katharine wouldn't object; I know she wouldn't.

When Angie called John the night I miscarried, he said he knew the baby wouldn't make it. He didn't know how or why, he just knew. When he came home he had to make burial plans for a daughter he never saw and console a wife who was inconsolable. I blamed myself. Dr. Felix had warned me about toxemia and I had ignored him. I felt so happy, how could anything go wrong? John tried not to blame me, but he did. He tried to be supportive, but he wasn't. He buried himself in work. Then he went on a couple of hunting trips with our station's general manager. I wouldn't eat the pheasant they'd shot. I couldn't. I abhorred hunting and John knew it. He stopped going after I protested.

Months later accusation was still in his eyes, and in his voice.

"Why didn't you listen to the doctor, Laura? He told you to take it easy, for God sakes!"

I had no answer for him, only the feeling that I . . .we . . . could have prevented this terrible, terrible thing. But didn't John want me to earn some money as long as possible? Wasn't he the one who worried about losing half our income?

That's when it started. After our baby, Jennifer Wells Newton, disappeared from our lives, having brushed by us for a short eight prenatal months and an impossible two minutes. That's when the cracks in the foundation of our marriage started.

I return the letters in my lap to their home piles. The already-read bunch. The two-lives-re-lived cluster. I'm hungry, for what I don't know. I'll think about it later. For now I must keep going, must keep re-living, I think, as I reach for more.

4/15/82

Dear Katharine,

Thank you for this beautiful journal. I'm so touched by it. I love the feel of its uneven black vinyl surface and the look of the embossed gold design on the front and spine. The white blank pages inside smell of virgin paper. They reflect the state I find myself in, empty and blank. Maybe returning to work so quickly wasn't such a good idea. I get into fights with everybody. I'm short-tempered, snap at people—the production assistants, our associate director, the stage manager, and even Peter who is the best boss I've ever worked for. He's been so tolerant of my mood swings. John and I've little to say to each other. We both stay at work later and later. We don't have to talk that way. He, in the business office, and me, in the production office just down the hall. We might as well be in separate countries.

I'm glad you're feeling well. It's so important for you to eat right—healthy foods, protein, fruit, vegetables. There I go again.

Don't pay attention to me. I can't help it. I want everything to be right for you. Thank you for being there, in the hospital I mean. Bringing me those strawberries was the best thing you could've done, besides holding my hand. Why can't I cry?

    Love, me

Happy Birthday!!!!
April 24, 1982
Santa Barbara

Dear Laura,
I know you wanted to ignore your birthday this year, but you know I will never forget. It has been almost twenty years since we met. I celebrate that meeting and wish this year to be a healing time for you and John.
The baby kicks and keeps me awake. I crochet baby booties through the night, twelve pairs so far.
"Yes, my child, tomorrow the daisies will grow tall as redwood trees."
Joseph Pintauro

Love always, Katharine

P.S. Have you written in the journal?

**SOMEONE NEW
HAS ARRIVED IN OUR LIVES:
JILLIAN GAY FIELDS
ON
JULY 30, 1982
9 LBS. 4 OZ.
21 INCHES
DADDY AND BABY ARE DOING FINE.
MOMMY IS TOO!**

August 13, 1982
Santa Barbara

Dear Laura,

She is so pretty. Blue eyes, cleft chin like her dad, thin lips like mine, "skin as white as snow." The palms of her little hands are like crushed rose petals.

My energy returns slowly. After thirty hours of labor, Jillian was born healthy and howling. No, I did not want the c-section, but I failed to progress. I was so out-of-it towards the end there are parts that are vague. Sorry I do not remember your phone call. David and I walked the hospital corridors all night because with each contraction I needed to move.

David is so proud, handing out lollipops to everyone. He is in complete awe of our creation. So am I.

Yes, please come up and see her. I am glad you decided to after all. If you change your mind at the last minute, I will understand.

Katharine and I are upstairs, bent over the wash basin in the bathroom. We're giggling and talking baby-ese to a little droplet of life that fits within her aquamarine shell-shaped sink perfectly, like Thumbelina. Jillian Fields is six weeks old. Jennifer Newton would have been over six months old if . . .

"That's my baby, that's a good girl," Katharine coos. I hand her a white towel with pink gingham piping as she lifts all eleven pounds of Jillian out of her bath. Katharine slips the corner of the towel that's shaped like a pocket over her baby's head. Jillian gives us both a look of wonder, her cheeks pink, her lips pursed in the shape of the letter O. Katharine hands the baby to me and Jillian starts to protest a little as I lean her upright against my shoulder. I feel the softness of her tiny face against mine. I support her head with my hand placed at the back, to prevent it from flopping around. She feels like a cake of Dove soap—soft and creamy. She smells of baby oil. This is what I've been missing. This tiny burst of life, my own little piece of which does not belong to my present, nor my past, nor perhaps my future?

Jillian is crying and rooting for her mother. I hand her back to Katharine as it's time to nurse her. I make some Raspberry Leaf Tea for us both. While waiting for the water to boil I sit on the edge of the bed. Katharine rocks back and forth in a worn, second-hand oak rocker David bought at a garage sale. It's hard to tell that David's auto repair shop is next door. It's so still up here in the bedroom. Jillian hungrily sucks her mother's milk. We both laugh as we hear the loud gulps. It seems impossible that such a small delicate thing can make such a vociferous sound. The tea kettle's shrill note calls me down to the kitchen.

Moments later, I climb the stairs back up to the bedroom. I reach the last step and look toward the rocker. I see Katharine—her head leaning against the back of the rocker, hair the color of straw barely caressing her shoulders, eyes closed, breasts exposed, veins bulging across her chest, royal blue thoroughfares set against white translucent skin. She appears captivated in a sensuous dream, her blush-colored lips slightly parted. Jillian's eyes are closed, jaws working, enveloped in a dream of bliss. These two women are bonded together by the ecstasy of this moment. I feel excluded, left behind, an intruder in this expression of motherhood. I'm aroused as I watch, but this feeling gives awkwardness to my movements and I almost drop the rattan tray. I carefully set down our clear glass mugs on the desk and pour the tea—the color of untouched amber. It's hot and steaming, and so am I. Katharine opens her eyes and looks at me with those lakes of blue. I long to share in this life-giving act with her. I want to cry, but I can't. I can't cry. Nurturing—will I ever know it in this utterly feminine way?

We sit together, in silence, sipping our hot tea as we watch Jillian consume the nectar that's still flowing from her mother's breasts. The tea burns my lips and tongue as it enters my body. I say nothing, but I want more.

Chapter Nine:
More

Laura Wells' Journal

July 17, 1989
Vista del Mar Inn
Santa Barbara
8:30 p.m.

"Yes, John . . . okay . . . yes . . . I know." His voice sounds urgent, pleading even. He says that he loves me at least twice in the span of fifteen minutes. That's a new record for him. "All right . . . I promise . . . . well, I talked to Katharine's friend at the hospital and she said—" He keeps putting me on hold.

"Yeah and what happened?" he rushes me.

"Before that I talked to Katharine's aunt, remember her? I forgot she even lived up here."

"Hold on. Sorry babe, it's another problem with that fucking show and it's costing about a million per episode. Damn that bozo VP who okayed it—"

"John, I can't keep doing this."

"What?"

"Being put on hold."

"Laura, come on, that's bullshit and you know it . . . oh shit . . . I've got to take this, we'll talk when you get home, you *are* coming home, yes? Late supper tonight at our favorite place, you can tell me everything, okay?"

"Okay." Although I know nothing's okay. It never is with John. There won't be any dinner; there won't be any space for me or my tale. It's always that way. He runs his division because showbiz is his life and he loves it. I get what's left and now it's not enough. Telling me he loves me and then putting me on hold as he always does is not enough. I just can't hold on any longer. And now I don't have to.

I wanted to give John the good news, but he was too busy. I wanted to tell him that I finally spoke with Sherry from Outside/Inside Books. I wanted to tell him that my collection of short stories won their cash prize of $10,000 and will be published next year. I hoped that acknowledgement would force him to finally hear me, but most likely he'd have already pushed the hold button before I'd gotten past the words "Sherry from—." John can't help it, that's his calling, putting out fires, putting the kibosh on projects that don't serve the studio's purpose and spinning the numbers for those that do. It's what drives him.

Meanwhile, he's putting out another fire, already just smoldering embers: my onetime love for him.

It was only a few hours ago I was standing at the front door of David's house. Irene answered when I knocked. Irene—my God, I didn't even know she was still alive. When Katharine's parents died, she was a great support to Katharine, or so she told me. She was really Katharine's mother's aunt, Katharine's great aunt, but she was always called Neny by Katharine and her mother, and now by Jillian. No one answered my quiet tapping on the brass figure of a female hand clutching the knocker, not at first. Katharine and I had found it while antique shopping one day on State Street in Santa Barbara. Neny opened the door and walked out: she was leaving and locking up the house. David's car repair shop was closed too. I forgot it was always closed on Mondays.

"Laura, is that you?" She later she told me she was seventy-eight, but she looked ten years younger, with no hint of gray in her upswept red hair. We embraced as we hadn't seen each other since Katharine and I were in college and I was amazed that she remembered me. "You haven't changed a bit, dear." I wanted to believe her kindness, but I knew I had changed, especially in these last few days, and I was sad to think it didn't show. "I mean, you don't look any older now than you did then, why look at you!" She gave me a gentle pat on the cheek. Although I didn't really know her as I'd only seen her a few times at Katharine's parents' apartment, I was sure she meant well.

Neny lived a bus ride away and had promised to check on the house for David.

"What do you mean, check on the house? Where is everyone?"

"David's girlfriend lives up in Monterey, so he and Jillian went up there for the week to get away from this sad, sad business," she said, looking down at the ground and shaking her head from side to side.

"I just stopped by to say goodbye. I'm going back home later tonight and I . . . I wanted to—" Tears filled my eyes. David's substitute for Katharine had already replaced her. My nose was running. I reached for a tissue, Neny handed me her hand-embroidered hanky. It smelled of Chanel Number 5. I'd always hated that cologne ever since the girl who stole Tony away from me in high school wore it, but I accepted Neny's handkerchief gratefully and wept even harder into it. I remember Katharine said Neny embroidered everything herself and used to teach the craft to young ladies, but that was long ago. She was quite refined in her designs, and Katharine liked them so much she had had a collection of Neny's exquisite hankies—a gift for high school graduation, which was supposed to have been saved for Jillian. I felt awkward wiping away my tears and snot on such finery.

I turned to walk back to my car and decided to say nothing about the box in the trunk I was attempting to return. Neny had been out of town when Katharine died and had missed the wake. Neny asked me for a ride home. I really wanted to know what she thought of this whole unhappy business and off we went in the late-afternoon light.

"Earl Grey is my favorite at this time of day . . . just gives me enough of a kick to make dinner later." As Neny poured me a cup and then one for herself, she confirmed for me all the snippets of conversation I had heard at the wake: Katharine's last days were filled with obsessive-compulsive phone calls to everyone in the family who would listen. Neny had refused to take her calls anymore.

We sat on Neny's white sofa with black dragons emblazoned across the cushions displaying her love for all things oriental. Black-lacquered Chinese end tables stood like sentries on the two sides of the couch and a Labradorite Kuan Yin statue, the Chinese Goddess of Mercy, sat on top of her crackled burnt orange square coffee table. A reproduction of a delicate Chinese scroll representing a panda among bamboo hung above her mantle. It was a small and cozy apartment made spacious by the dynamics of her Far East interior decorating. A landscape design shoji screen divided the kitchen/dining area from the small living room. The coved ceilings gave the place a sense of width and breadth that most studio apartments lacked. I felt quite at home as Neny's demeanor absorbed my need to discover more truth and yet the mystique of the décor compelled me to be inquisitive and just come out with that one burning question that had plagued me since my immersion in the past had almost swallowed me up.

"Neny, do you think Katharine's molestation all those years ago was part of this?" She reached over and poured cream in her tea and stirred it for several moments before answering. "I mean, I remember something about that, but was it really true?" Again I preferred not to say how I knew.

"Oh Laura, one thing you had to remember about Katharine was that she was such a sensitive child. She talked with me just before her first breakdown and she claimed that when she was on vacation with her parents at the family home in Oregon 'something' had happened up in the attic with her father. She wouldn't say what, but she described for me the attic and some old family boxes that were stored there, and she cried and insisted again *something* had happened. And that every time she returned there, that 'something' continued to occur. She was so upset I didn't have the heart to tell her that that particular house had no attic, but it did have a small root cellar. And that her father had never been back after he and Betty married. That was my parents' old place and my daughter lived there until she died, and she and Betty were estranged.

"You must remember also, my dear, that Katharine loved to write. My goodness, I remember her mother saving all these scraps of papers, oodles of them, don't you know, that Katharine had scrawled stories on as a child and then thrown away. I don't think Katharine knew that Betty had saved them. But she was always very very imaginative. Even after her sister and the children died in that horrid crash, little Katharine was so heartbroken that she wrote many short stories and poems about her. They weren't true of course, as Katharine wrote about how Bett lived through the crash and grew to a ripe old age of 30, I guess that was old to a ten-year-old, and how Bett and she became expert balloonists flying all over the world rescuing all the little orphans and whisking them off to safety in their big yellow balloon."

I swallowed the wrong way, spilling most of my tea and burning the tops of my thighs. Between coughing and spurting, wiping up the mess, and apologizing for making such a muddle, my head was swirling. "It's all right, dear, you're probably in quite the state, I imagine. I know I was, but I saw this coming and, well . . . Katharine is in a better place isn't she, mind you, it's so sad for Jillian, but in the last year Katharine was terrifying for that little girl to be around, spouting off about the devil and evil and dying. I mean, we have to think about Jillian now, don't we? I mean David and his new lady do, and trust me, she is very sweet—and she looks a bit like Katharine. The good thing is, she seems to care a great deal for the child."

I needed to get out of there. I just wanted to run out the door. And I rose so abruptly that I almost knocked over the Chinese Goddess of Mercy on my way out, spluttering with excuses about avoiding traffic and having to make a couple more stops before heading back to L.A. to meet my husband. One of those stops had to be the southwest side of Santa Barbara to see Maria, the woman who'd spoken to me so briefly through such tears at the wake.

Incongruous, I think, that Katharine was unable to call on the goddess of mercy for compassion as she certainly received none from her own family.

I check the map the hotel concierge gave me earlier, and head over to the hospital. The nurse on the phone had said to head about six blocks toward State Street and that the hospital would be down a side street east of the main drag. She warned me it was in a very un-hospital-like area, industrial she said, and indeed it looks more like the auto dismantling capital of Santa Barbara. One after another funky antiquated and surly auto repair and body shop lines Haley Street. No wonder David never moved here. He liked the home and the shop combined into a one-stop shop.

"I'm here to see Maria, please," I blurt, announcing myself to the receptionist. The place is colorless, shabby, and anonymous. White walls marred by chipped paint where empty metal brown folding chairs line the reception area, in two rows of five. The navy blue faded carpet is torn just in front of the reception area. I recall David saying he had filled out papers to make Katharine a ward of the state. I didn't realize what he'd meant until now. This place smells of forgotten memories and stale cigarettes. Empty Styrofoam coffee cups overflow out of a black plastic wastebasket no one has bothered to clean out. Visiting hours end at 8 o'clock and it's 7:15, so I don't have much time.

"I remember you that day at the wake, your eyes were so soft," Maria says, smiling with her large black eyes as we sit around a bare plastic orange circular table in the small empty dining room that doubles as a meeting room. Unlike Maria's conservative black dress at the wake, tonight she wears a purple turtleneck that partially hides a green and red tattoo that looks like the end of a mermaid's tail peeping out from her neck, but I'm not sure. Her black matted hair looks like it's just been sliced off unevenly with a razor, but they probably don't allow those here. I decide not to ask. In fact, when I had asked the nurse if it was all right to come to visit Maria, I was told it would be allowed on the condition that I must not ask her too many personal questions. She becomes agitated when probed about why she is in the hospital or how long she has been a resident. The nurse only confirmed that Maria had lived here for almost a year. I decide to just compliment Maria on her baby blue nail polish and say it reminds me of the color of the ocean outside my hotel room that has comforted my life lived in rewind this week.

We take silent breaths while watching each other intently. We make some small talk. She tells me that Katharine always talked about me as someone who she really loved and depended on. Strangely, I don't feel like I filled that bill in the last months of Katharine's life. And it weighs on me like an iron maiden.

Maria holds her box of Marlboro Lights out to me and I can't resist. She asks me to get a light from the nearby nurses' station, so I do. Maria fingers the matchbook awkwardly as if she hasn't held one in a while, and has to strike two matches before they ignite from which we both puff madly, nervously, and then rapidly exhale out the sides of our mouths. I French inhale and she laughs at me. Maria does it also, but is more practiced than I am, apparently, and doesn't cough like I just did.

"Yes," I say, clearing my throat, "I saw you too, and tried to talk to you, but you left so fast."

"Yeah, that was Paul's doing."

"Paul?"

"Our counselor, he said we had to go, he thought I was losin' it, you know, with my waterworks and all. He runs group here and is the one who drove us to our picnic that day Katharine disapp—walked away."

"What do you mean, walked away?"

"She said she was going to."

"Where . . . why didn't anyone stop her then?"

"It's all my fault. Paul says it's not. And I know that now, but I still can't help feeling it is."

"You mean stopping her, or letting her go?"

"Katharine was racked with guilt about the way her life had gone to shit. She blamed herself for David's turning away from her; she blamed herself for alienating Jillian. She talked about it in group all the time. No matter what we all said, that it wasn't her fault, that she was sick and that no one blamed her, Katharine didn't wanna hear it. Her persecution complex was a mothafucking Medusa. Katharine told me that once in a dream she'd stared into the face of that goddess and had seen past the veil, and that Medusa had shown her that her death was near."

"Near how?"

"Katharine said that she had no more illusions about the rest of her life—it was time, she said, to cross that threshold and do it without fear."

"So she just left on her own? She wasn't lost then? She made—"

"She made a decision that morning on the way to the lake. I saw it in her eyes. She'd been telling me . . . all of us in group, that she was on the approach, and a hunger gnawing at her to cross over was like a calling. And then she caught a bad bout of flu . . . but she faked feeling better just to get on that bus.

"But how could she just abandon Jillian like that?" I take a drag and try to calm my voice from shouting. I know Katharine would never have walked away from her daughter so callously. She couldn't have.

Maria looks me in the eye and spits out "Listen, you didn't know her like I do . . . did." Anger flushes across my face, the red spreads to the back of my neck. This woman had only known her less than a year! And yet she knew something I had missed. I puff on what's left of my stub of a cigarette and put it out, pissed off like I'm the only one here who didn't get the memo about Katharine.

"That little girl came a couple times to visit her after Katharine was brought here, but in the last months Katharine scared her away. She had stopped washing and eating. She'd lost so much weight that her doctor forced her to go to the hospital once to feed her intravenously. She was a skeleton, but she wanted it that way. Then in the middle of the night she'd rave about the devil and needing to die, so they upped her sleeping meds. That husband of hers never brought Jillian back, hell, the asshole never came back either. Katharine didn't abandon Jillian, she made a sacrifice for her!" Maria's voice booms in my face as she wipes away her tears.

I wipe away mine also, those relentless tears that refuse switching off since I arrived in Santa Barbara. Maria calls to the nurse to bring us back some matches as I had returned them to the nurse's station because Maria told me we aren't really allowed to keep them in here. This time the nurse lights us up and leaves. We sit and puff and stare, sometimes at each other, sometimes just into the space between us.

"But Katharine was ill, none of this was her fault," I say, between hiccups of more tears.

"Katharine wasn't *that* crazy in those last days, more like fox-crazy," Maria insists. "She was in pain, that's all; she had a seeping wound that wouldn't quit. No amount of meds or therapy can squelch that kind of fucking agony. She knew it would never go away, she knew she would never stop being blamed by her husband for destroying their lives, even though he had plenty to do with it and wouldn't admit it."

"I'll never forgive him for pushing her away," I said, blowing my nose.

"She let him in the end because of Jillian . . . plus that new girlfriend of David's came here just a couple weeks before Katharine died."

"She did! What for?"

"Katharine wouldn't tell me much, but she seemed at peace after their conversation. I was in the dining room that day helping set up lunch. They let me work that shift when an employee called in sick. I used to be a waitress once," she adds, then her words trail off for a moment. She puffs a bit, thinks a bit, blows out more smoke and continues, "and I heard something the chick said about how she loved little Jillian too and that she'd never forget and not to worry 'cause everything would be okay. That was all I could catch since the cook made me go back to the kitchen and help wash dishes."

It's almost 8 o'clock and I'm informed that visiting hours are over. I thank Maria for talking to me and she reaches out to hug me goodbye. I hug her back tightly as this is one of the last people to see my Katharine alive. Maria then whispers in my ear, "One more thing." I stand back and look into her eyes, and she says, "That other woman." I'm not sure at first whom she means, then of course I realize she means David's girlfriend.

"Yes, what about her?"

"Funny thing was she and Katharine looked like they could have been sisters, they had the same color hair and the same blue eyes, only Katharine's hair, that day, was long and straggly and this other chick's was cut short, or maybe it was just piled up on her head, but I'm not—"

We're abruptly cut off by a pug-faced nurse whose name tag reads Charlotte, although I prefer Nurse Ratched because as I start to ask another question, she sternly insists that I leave, pointing me to the door. "It's time," she says with cold eyes, and escorts Maria down a hall as we wave goodbye. Shit. I want another cigarette, but Maria takes her pack. I decide it's all for the best, the cigarettes, I mean. The rest, I'm not so sure. I don't want to believe what Maria has said. Katharine's sister was long dead. And yet Maria's words bring up the specter of a sister reincarnated somehow. I realize this can't be, but at the same time I wish it were true. As I start the car and head south toward the 101 I think how desperately every baby deserves and needs its mother, but is the best mother always the biological one?

The night lays itself down across the highway as I head back, leaving the Pacific coast and driving inland. What now? John waits, but that doesn't bother me so much, I've waited for him to see me all these years, truly see me as I am now. In this new light I see myself slantwise and the fit feels awkward, but it will work its way into a new and more empowered form.

Sherry and I are meeting next week to talk about my collection of short stories that she likes so much. She asked if I have any more work I would consider submitting for a new imprint that she and her partner have begun. I told her we'd talk about it at our lunch meeting.

Maybe I do.

I carry them in the trunk of my car, I carry them at the center of my heart, I carry them for Katharine's sake and Jillian's. I know that I can carry them aloft for others to be enriched by stories of remembrance, loss, and liberation, something with a simple but meaningful title . . . The Katharine Stories.

About the Author

Linda Rader Overman holds a Master of Fine Arts in Creative Writing from California State University, Chico. *Letters Between Us* was a finalist in literary achievement at the Pacific Northwest Writers Conference and is her debut novel. Her work has appeared in *Chican@s in the Conversations, Talking River, Hands Across Borders, Pacific Coast Philology, Voices, onthebus*, among others. Currently, she teaches English at California State University, Northridge.

Letters Between Us was selected as a "Finalist in Fiction & Literature: Chick Lit/Women's Lit" category of the National Best Books 2008 Awards, sponsored by USA Book News. Her website is http://lindaraderoverman.com.

Printed in the United States
129036LV00001B/2/P